"You w

The jutting of Lydia's chin only proved that she felt every inch of his stare. "I know."

"And it's not in my interests to keep it secret."

"A month. That's all I'm asking for. A month."

"I will give you a week."

"But..."

"A week or nothing." Alexis made to walk away.

"Fine," she snapped. "A week. But a week from the wedding."

"Deal." He gave a mocking smile. "Our first compromise."

"Hardly a compromise."

"You should be more grateful—I didn't need to compromise. I don't need to compromise on anything. That we're standing here even discussing this is entirely for your benefit."

"No, for our *baby's* benefit."

"Once you know me better, you will know our baby's security was never in doubt."

"If it wasn't for our baby, I wouldn't want to know you at all."

"But you, my angel from hades, do know me, and *intimately*." He had the satisfaction of her beautiful face contorting at the reminder.

A brand-new enthralling Harlequin Presents duet from Michelle Smart.

Greek Rivals

Two opposing families... Two forbidden passions?

Thanasis Antoniadis and Alexis Tsaliki are fierce competitors. The feud between their families has been raging in Greece for decades—and it's driving both their billion-euro shipping empires into the ground. They need to find a way to save their families' fortunes and put an end to this conflict. So falling for women who are their sworn enemies is the last thing either of them needs...

Thanasis agrees to marry Lucie, Alexis's stepsister, to end the rumors of hostility. When an accident leaves Lucie with no memory of their convenient engagement, Thanasis has no choice but to keep up the fiancée facade. And to keep his distance from the enemy he's dangerously tempted by!

Read Thanasis and Lucie's story in
Forgotten Greek Proposal

Lydia Antoniadis is the last woman Alexis should be sharing a sizzling night with. No one is more off-limits than his rival's sister! And neither could have anticipated that their recklessly passionate encounter would have such shocking and life-changing consequences...

Discover Alexis and Lydia's story in
His Pregnant Enemy Bride

Both available now!

HIS PREGNANT ENEMY BRIDE

MICHELLE SMART

Harlequin
PRESENTS

If you purchased this book without a cover you should be aware that this book is stolen property. It was reported as "unsold and destroyed" to the publisher, and neither the author nor the publisher has received any payment for this "stripped book."

Harlequin® PRESENTS™

ISBN-13: 978-1-335-21318-1

His Pregnant Enemy Bride

Copyright © 2025 by Michelle Smart

All rights reserved. No part of this book may be used or reproduced in any manner whatsoever without written permission.

Without limiting the author's and publisher's exclusive rights, any unauthorized use of this publication to train generative artificial intelligence (AI) technologies is expressly prohibited.

This is a work of fiction. Names, characters, places and incidents are either the product of the author's imagination or are used fictitiously. Any resemblance to actual persons, living or dead, businesses, companies, events or locales is entirely coincidental.

For questions and comments about the quality of this book, please contact us at CustomerService@Harlequin.com.

TM and ® are trademarks of Harlequin Enterprises ULC.

Harlequin Enterprises ULC
22 Adelaide St. West, 41st Floor
Toronto, Ontario M5H 4E3, Canada
www.Harlequin.com

Printed in Lithuania

Michelle Smart's love affair with books started when she was a baby and would cuddle them in her cot. A voracious reader of all genres, she found her love of romance established when she stumbled across her first Harlequin book at the age of twelve. She's been reading them—and writing them—ever since. Michelle lives in Northamptonshire, England, with her husband and two young smarties.

Books by Michelle Smart

Harlequin Presents

Innocent's Wedding Day with the Italian
Christmas Baby with Her Ultra-Rich Boss
Cinderella's One-Night Baby
Resisting the Bossy Billionaire
Spaniard's Shock Heirs

A Billion-Dollar Revenge

Bound by the Italian's "I Do"

The Greek Groom Swap

The Forbidden Greek

The Diamond Club

Heir Ultimatum

Greek Rivals

Forgotten Greek Proposal

Visit the Author Profile page at Harlequin.com for more titles.

CHAPTER ONE

Lydia Antoniadis peered intently through the binoculars she'd borrowed from a deckhand, watching the supply boat heading in the direction of Kos. She'd caught a fleeting glance at a figure slipping below deck, which in itself was not in the least strange, but what was strange was that the figure bore a strong resemblance to Lucie Burton. But it couldn't be Lucie because Lucie was marrying Lydia's brother the next day on Sephone and so definitely wouldn't be sailing away from the island. It must have been a trick of the mind. After all, the distance between the yacht Lydia stood on the sundeck of and the supply boat was immense.

Definitely a mind trick, she assured herself again before training the binoculars on Sephone itself. The island's gorgeous multiple-domed villa was gleaming under the rising sun, and she slowly scanned the faces in its front grounds. The only ones she recognised were the household staff, which wasn't really surprising considering it was barely nine a.m. They all looked stressed, which wasn't surprising either considering hundreds of people were about to descend on the island for the wedding. Most would be there before nightfall.

Draining her glass of water, she looked out again over the Aegean. More vessels had appeared since she'd become distracted by the figure on the supply boat.

'You're up early, *baba*.'

Lydia flinched but didn't drop the binoculars. 'I didn't hear you sneak up on me.'

'I was hardly sneaking,' her mother said drily, standing beside her at the balustrade. 'What's got you so enraptured?'

'Nothing. Just looking to see if I recognise any of the yachts heading this way.'

'And?'

'Too far away to tell. Looks like we'll be the third party to arrive.' There were two superyachts already anchored, and they sailed past them, the crew scurrying around preparing to dock at the small harbour that could accommodate only two vessels. Lydia's brother refused to dredge the shoreline of his precious island to accommodate more.

'Are any of *them* here yet?'

Them. Meaning the Tsalikis.

Lydia's fingers tightened but her voice remained steady. 'No.'

'Good. I couldn't face seeing any of them before my breakfast has been digested. Have you eaten?'

'I'll get something later.' Her stomach was so tightly knotted she'd struggled to get water into it.

'You need to eat.'

'Don't fuss. I'm fine.'

'None of us are fine, *baba*, but we all need to eat. It's going to be a long couple of days and we need to keep our strength up.'

Lydia nodded automatically. Since their lives had imploded her mother had gone into self-preservation mode with a steely smile and a steelier determination that whatever happened to the family business and fortune, the family itself would survive. Part of this survival came in the form of food. Her mother had always been a feeder but in recent months, Lydia had been unable to walk through the front door without having food thrust in her face. What they had travelled to Sephone for, though, was going to push her mother's steely smile to the limit: a marriage between Lydia's brother Thanasis and Lucie Burton, the stepdaughter of their enemy Georgios Tsaliki. For the next three days, with the world's press acting as witnesses, they were going to break bread, smile, dance and laugh with their heinous sworn enemy and his equally heinous family. This wedding was the Antoniadises' last chance to save their business and save themselves from destitution.

Soon, their yacht was moored beside Thanasis's and it was time to disembark and play their parts in the performance of the century. With her father striding along the jetty as if he'd spent his whole lifetime waiting impatiently for this wedding and her mother striding purposefully with her steely smile fixed firmly in place, Lydia followed behind them, attempting her own steely smile and trying her hardest not to think that the one thing that could actually break her mother lay nestled in her stomach.

Alexis Tsaliki read the message Thanasis Antoniadis had sent him for a third time, spat a curse, and pressed the intercom. 'Get the jet ski out for me. Now.'

Jumping out of bed, he threw shorts, a T-shirt and a pair of running shoes on, then raced out of his yacht's master cabin and banged on his father's door. His stomach curdled when his stepmother opened it but there was no time for unpleasantries. 'Where is he?'

'Showering. What's wrong?'

He pushed past her without answering and banged on the bathroom door. 'Dad, get out of there. We need to talk.'

'What's wrong?' his stepmother asked again.

Not bothering to hide the loathing he usually masked for the sake of family harmony, he said tightly, 'Your daughter.' Then he banged even louder on the bathroom door.

'Lucie? What's happened?'

'Dad!' he shouted. 'We need to talk right now.'

The bathroom door opened and Alexis was engulfed in a cloud of steam and the unedifying sight of his father dripping wet from the shower he'd been enjoying. 'What's wrong?'

'Lucie knows everything. She's gone. The wedding's off.'

His father seemed to deflate before his eyes.

'What do you mean *she's gone*?' Rebecca demanded in a high voice. 'How can she be *gone*?'

One of his siblings—and Alexis had many siblings—having heard the commotion, barged into the cabin, quickly followed by another and another and another until it seemed like every Tsaliki in existence was in the cabin shouting over each other, all throwing panicked questions at him.

'That's all I know!' he roared over the noise. 'Everyone get dressed. We'll be anchoring soon and you can take the tender over, but I'm taking the jet ski there now so I can find out exactly what's going on and see if I can find Lucie and talk some sense into her.'

Not giving them the chance to argue, he elbowed his way out of the cabin.

The jet ski was ready for him. Throwing himself on it, he turned the engine on and, not caring that he wore no life jacket, set off at top speed to Sephone.

Lydia saw the figure speeding to the island on the jet ski before anyone else. No trickery caused by distance could discount what the thumping of her heart was telling her, and she gripped her forearms and swallowed back a swell of nausea that was different from the nausea already rolling in her stomach.

'It will be okay, *baba*,' her father said, noticing the change in her demeanour and wrapping a trembling arm around her. Kissing the top of her head, he whispered, 'I promise, everything will be okay.'

She leaned into him, fighting the threatening tears

and fighting the growing urge to open her lungs and vocal cords and just scream; scream until her throat was raw and she had no breath left to give.

'Thanasis will fix it,' her father added, as if Lydia's brother were a god amongst mortals and could bend the world to his whim.

'How?' she whispered dully. 'Lucie will never marry him now. It's over. Everything's over.'

She looked at her mother slumped on the fine white sand, the steely smile wiped off her face, her expression that of utter despair. Looked at her brother sitting on the same rock he'd been propped on when he'd explained the situation to them, her mighty big brother who always had the answer to everything sitting there as if all his stuffing had been knocked out of him. And then she glanced again at the figure on the jet ski closing in on the beach.

Another swell of nausea rose from the pit of her stomach followed by a swell of anguished fury and, without thinking of what she was doing, she wrenched herself out of her father's comforting hold and rounded on her brother.

'What the hell were you thinking, lying to Lucie like that?'

His dull eyes barely focussed on hers. His confession had left him spent.

Nearly two weeks ago, Lucie had been in a car crash that had seen her hospitalised for days with a major head injury. Thanasis had brought her to his private island to recover. It had made sense. Sephone was a tranquil Greek paradise and their wedding was being held there. Unbeknownst to Lydia, her parents and the rest of the world, Lucie's accident had been caused after she'd called the wedding off and fled Thanasis's Athens apartment. Unbeknownst to them all too, Lucie's head injury had caused an amnesia. She'd forgotten everything about the wedding, including the huge row that had seen her flee from Thanasis. Between them, Thanasis, Lucie's mother, stepfather and the oldest of her stepbrothers, Alexis, had conspired to make Lucie believe that, far from hating each other, she and Thanasis had fallen in love for real and not just as a game being played out for the sake of their respective family businesses' survival.

'Lydia, don't,' her mother said tiredly. 'Your brother is suffering enough.'

Usually her mother's warning would be enough to make Lydia shut up, but in that moment too many emotions were crowding in her head and chest, and her heart was thrashing too wildly at the jet ski figure closing in on them for her to listen or think clearly.

'*He's* suffering?' she screamed. 'Well, I'm glad! It serves him right! Lucie did *nothing* to deserve being treated like that.' Her back to the sea, she threw her hands on her hips to stop them lashing out at her zombified brother. 'She gave up her home and career to save our business and you did *that* to her?'

Because the engagement and planned wedding had never been real. Her father's uncivil war with his old friend and former business partner turned enemy, Georgios Tsaliki, had escalated to the degree that

Georgios had sabotaged the engines of their cargo fleet and Lydia's father had retaliated by having millions of cockroaches and rats let loose in Georgios's own fleet. What had been treated in the press as an amusing rivalry between two rival shipping magnates had overnight become a scandal that had ballooned as old dirty tricks between them were either brought to light or rehashed with a brand-new slant. The scandal had led to Antoniadis Shipping's main investors threatening to pull their money. If acted on, Antoniadis Shipping would go bankrupt.

Tsaliki Shipping hadn't gone unscathed either. Whilst not fatally wounded like the Antoniadises were close to being, its share prices had plummeted and, with no sign of recovery on the horizon, it was agreed that the only way to manage the situation and prove that the next generation were now in charge and that all the bad blood between the two families was over, was through marriage. Petros Antoniadis's son Thanasis would marry Georgios Tsaliki's beloved stepdaughter Lucie.

Except it had been a match made in hell. Thanasis had been determined to hate Lucie and she in turn had grown to despise him.

Poor Lucie had thought Thanasis's love for her was true and had opened her heart to him.

Lydia didn't have to stretch her imagination very far to imagine how devastated Lucie must have felt to learn the truth and learn that she'd been so cruelly played and her injury weaponised against her.

'He did what he had to do to save us all,' her mother defended.

'Well, he didn't save us, did he?' she cried. 'My honourable brother who never lies...' She shook her head in disgust. 'You men, you're all the same. You lie and you lie and you lie, and now you have the nerve to sit there looking all injured and sorry for yourself? You caused this, Thanasis. *You*. If you'd bothered to take me into your confidence instead of listening to that bastard Alexis, I would have told you not to do it. I would have told you to level with her and now look what we're left with!'

'I will find her and I will bring her back here. She will listen to me.'

The voice had come from behind her, its impact freezing her on the spot.

He'd reached them.

Like synchronised meerkats, her mother, brother and father all looked over her shoulder.

Lydia wasn't sure if time really did stand still or if the roar of blood in her head made it seem that way, but in the time it took her to turn to face him, no one spoke.

She looked at the man she'd last seen in the flesh naked, and came within a breath of vomiting on the spot. Summoning every ounce of her strength, she raised herself as tall as she could draw her short, curvy figure and crossed her arms. Then and only then did she meet the stare that had once melted her bones, and transferred all her anguish and loathing to him. 'You will leave her alone.'

The blue-grey eyes held hers for the beat of a moment before snapping away from her. 'Where is she?'

'Gone,' Thanasis replied in the same dull tone.

'Where? How did she find out? Did her memories come back?'

'I told her.'

'You…' The full, sensuous lips that had kissed Lydia senseless opened and closed as Alexis Tsaliki's handsome face contorted in disbelief. 'You told her? What the…?'

'She needed to know.'

'No, she needed to damn well marry you! Have you lost your mind?'

'Yes.'

'Where is she?'

No one answered. Lucie thought of the supply boat heading towards Kos and the figure she'd seen slip below deck and said, 'Wherever she's gone, it doesn't matter. She doesn't want to marry Thanasis and that's the end of it.'

He didn't even look at her. 'Do you see all those yachts entering your waters, Thanasis? They are your guests. Your wedding guests. The press are on their way here too. If we don't get her back right now it will be too late.'

'It's already too late,' Lydia spat. 'Lucie doesn't want to marry him and I don't blame her.'

It was as if her voice didn't exist to his ears. His attention still on Thanasis, he said, 'I can think of a few places she would go. I'll get people on it. If you can—'

'No.' Thanasis's inertia lifted off him like a blanket as he rose to his feet. 'No. No search parties. We leave her alone. That's all she wants.'

'What's the matter with you? Who cares what she—?'

A roar cut Alexis's words off and then a split-second later he was on his back. Another split-second later and Thanasis was on top of him, his fist raised to land another punch, but this time Alexis was prepared and before Lydia could even blink, he'd flipped Thanasis onto his back, his own fist raised.

It was the scream that stopped Alexis from slamming his fist into Thanasis's face as the bastard deserved.

Breathing heavily, he pulled himself off him, wiped the blood seeping out of his lip with his thumb, and dusted himself down as he cast a disdainful eye over all the Antoniadises...except one. The one whose scream had stopped him giving as good as he'd been given.

'You're all finished. You understand that, yes? Everything you have...' He snapped his fingers together. 'In weeks it will all be gone. The losses my family have suffered will take time for me to recoup but I *will* recoup them, whereas you will have nothing to build back from because it will all be dust, and you will only have yourselves to blame.'

'And you,' said the voice he most hated, the voice whose scream had stopped him in his tracks. 'We will have you to blame too, and every member of your family that chose to lie and deceive a woman when she was at her most vulnerable. I don't know how you sleep at night.'

He tuned out the inflection of tone that suggested the speaker was talking about more than his stepsister. 'My conscience is clear,' he said tightly.

'That's because you don't actually have a conscience... Oh, look, here comes your family. How delightful. Is that really all the Tsaliki spawn squeezed on that tender? You should tell them to be careful—all those egos in one boat could make it capsize.'

Alexis took a long breath through his nose before fixing Lydia with a swift warning stare. 'Unless you want to lose any hope of salvaging something from this mess, I suggest you watch what you say about my family.'

She laughed. 'Or what? You'll bankrupt us? Those wheels will be turning as soon as the news breaks. We're finished, remember?'

'Damage limitation might buy you some time...' There was a tap on his shoulder. He turned to find Elektra Antoniadis's lined face gazing up at him.

He could almost feel sorry for the Antoniadis matriarch. Possibly he would have done if she hadn't been looking at him with such loathing.

'Threaten my daughter again and I will personally see to it that you never father children.'

He gave a bark of laughter. 'I didn't threaten your daughter, I warned her, in the spirit of friendship, not to use that cutting tongue of hers to slander my family. You still have time to prepare for damage limitation and I would have thought you would want me on side when you launch it—after all, you already know to your cost that my family makes a very bad enemy.'

The older woman didn't even blink, turning her long nose in the air and saying, 'More threats. We don't need or want your help or your *friendship*, and if my daughter chooses to use her cutting tongue to speak the truth about a family of degenerates then all I can say to that is that I wholeheartedly support her. Now come, *baba*. We have some damage limitation to be getting on with.'

To Alexis's surprise, Thanasis and his father had already walked away without him even noticing, and then his heart sank when Lydia shook her head and blew out the fringe from her eyes. 'I'll catch up with you—I've got some people I need to practise sharpening my tongue on.'

'Okay. Just don't get cut yourself.' Elektra eyed Alexis as she said that, then gave her daughter a kiss before hurrying after the two Antoniadis men.

Left alone with the one person he'd planned to actively avoid for the whole of his time spent on this damned island, Alexis clenched his jaw and kept his gaze fixed on the tender carrying his family across the sea to the jetty. 'You've obviously got something on your mind so whatever you've got to say to me, get it over with,' he said roughly. 'I've got my own damage limitation to be getting on with.'

'I'm pregnant.'

Her words didn't so much hang in the air as swing on a giant Newton's cradle, the silver balls knocking together to create a sudden deafening roar in his head.

'Say that again,' he dragged out.

'I'm pregnant.'

His chest tightened into an ice-cold ball. The pendulum swung again. Slowly, Alexis turned his head to face the woman standing beside him.

Her stare, what he could see of it beneath her enormous blonde fringe, was fixed ahead at the sea, her chin lifted, a picture of what would be serenity if not for the tremors racking her shoulders.

'You...' He had to swallow to speak. 'You are certain?'

'I had my first scan last week.'

'How...? Why...?' It was like he'd forgotten how to talk. 'Why have you waited all this time to tell me?'

'I wasn't going to tell you until the baby was born but Lucie running away changes everything. My job pays a pittance and my family are on the verge of bankruptcy so there is no way I can support the baby on my own now.'

There was a shout in the distance. He barely heard it, would have tuned it out completely if Lydia's stare hadn't flickered over to the direction it had come from. 'Your family are here. You should go to them. We can talk later. Don't mention the baby to anyone—I think everyone's got enough to be stressed about today. We can tell everyone once we're married.'

He'd barely picked his jaw up when the hazel eyes he'd never wanted to lock stares with again landed on him. 'I'm sorry, Alexis, but I won't have my child born into poverty. I need you to marry me.'

Her words had barely sunk in when she'd walked away and disappeared into the surrounding trees.

CHAPTER TWO

ONLY WHEN SHE was quite sure that she was hidden amongst the trees did Lydia put a hand to a trunk to steady herself and heave up all the water she'd consumed that morning. Perspiration had broken out all over her skin but she had nothing to blot her face with.

She was shaking, inside and out.

She'd known within a week of her night with Alexis that she'd conceived, known it before her period had failed to arrive. She hadn't told a soul outside the medical profession, had kept it a tightly held secret in her heart. A terrifying and yet miraculous secret. Terrifying because of how her family were going to react when they learned the identity of the father.

In the last six months or so Lydia had watched her parents age before her eyes, watched her father be removed from the company he'd founded and her brother installed in his place, and been subjected to a level of press intrusion she couldn't even bring herself to wish on the Tsalikis. The stress on everyone had been intolerable and she'd had no means to help, could only watch despairingly as her happy family began to disintegrate under the strain of it all.

She'd known the only way their family could rise before the business became ashes had been through forming a truce with the Tsalikis, something her parents had reacted to with fury when she'd suggested it. Her brother though... Thanasis had taken the idea with his usual thoughtful consideration. A seed had been planted. All she'd needed to do, so she'd figured, was plant another seed. The question had been how to plant that seed without her family finding out. The Greek shipping world was a world where nothing stayed secret. There was no way she could waltz into Tsaliki Shipping's headquarters and ask for a meeting without her parents finding out before she'd left the building. Even an innocuous email would be leaked, and so Lydia had dressed up in a nineteen-sixties-style silver mini dress and knee-high heeled boots, and taken herself to Alexis Tsaliki's favourite nightclub, the place he was regularly pictured spending his Friday nights.

Memories were funny things, she thought as she tried to breathe her body back under control. Some events passed and you looked back on them hardly able to remember a thing that had happened. With other events, every minute—*every second*—became etched in the memory...

Lydia had been to Athens' most exclusive nightclub only once before, years ago, for a friend's twenty-first birthday party. As with the first time, she climbed the wide, rounded stairs to the VIP section. This time she climbed them alone, and when she passed through the roped barrier, it was to a booth reserved for one. She'd used half her month's earnings to pay for this booth.

She gave it exactly fifteen minutes before carrying her champagne onto the dancefloor. Lydia loved dancing, but that night the only thing she had in mind was attracting Alexis Tsaliki's attention, and so she moved to the music keeping her stare fixed on the club's most private booth, the one most hidden in the shadows, where a tall, well-built man with perfectly quiffed hair so dark it was almost black was holding court with a harem of sycophants hanging onto his every word. Lydia would bet every woman at that table's skirt was shorter than her own, and she'd gone as short as she dared without giving both her parents a heart attack. If she wanted to attract his attention, she needed to look the part.

As she'd known would eventually happen, the eyes of the face she only knew from a distance drifted past her and then zoomed back. Their gazes locked. A flicker of recognition flared.

She raised her glass, smiled, and then sashayed off the dancefloor back to her booth.

Barely two minutes later, he slid into the booth beside her.

'Lydia Antoniadis,' he said, spreading out his long arms to rest along the top of the booth, taking a third of the available space. His cologne, a deliciously exotic scent that brought to mind untamed jungles, filled the rest of it.

'Alexis Tsaliki,' she replied with a sweet smile, refusing to be intimidated. But, wow, in person the man was even bigger than he'd looked from a distance, even taller and broader than her brother.

'And to what do I owe this pleasure?'

'Buy me a drink and I'll tell you.'

Blue-grey eyes that made her think of winter skies and yet weren't in the slightest bit cold narrowed almost imperceptibly before he beckoned a waitress and ordered two glasses of champagne.

'So, Lydia Antoniadis,' he said, settling back again and fixing his stare back on her. *'Tell me why the youngest member of the family at war with my family is here alone in my hunting ground.'*

She gave another sweet smile. *'Catching my prey, of course.'*

He leaned his face closer to hers, and what a face it was; not a single picture she'd seen of him over the years doing him the slightest bit of justice despite the camera loving him. *'And for what reason do you want to catch me, Lydia Antoniadis?'*

'To ask you, Alexis Tsaliki, to consider a truce.'

The beautiful eyes narrowed. *'Now why,'* he asked slowly, *'would I want to do that?'*

'Because all the negative headlines and publicity mean your company is suffering as much as ours?'

'I think you'll find that your company is in much worse shape than my father's. Or mine as it is now.' Alexis had recently taken control of his father's com-

pany. Rumour had it that he'd wrested it from him against his father's wishes.

Their champagne was delivered. Alexis handed Lydia's to her and then raised his own with a smile. 'Your father was too reliant on outside investment, which has made it much more vulnerable to external forces than mine.'

She clinked her glass to his. 'But all the negative publicity means Tsaliki Shipping is suffering a breakdown of consumer confidence as well as plummeting share prices. I understand you've lost three long-standing contracts in recent months.'

He had a drink of his champagne. 'I didn't think you were involved in Antoniadis Shipping.'

She swallowed half of her glass and smiled. 'I'm not. But I am an interested party. Obviously.'

'Obviously,' he echoed. 'An interested party close to losing everything.'

'You can stop that happening.'

A smile tugged at his mouth. She couldn't help thinking what divine lips they were, the perfect mouth with a fullness barely a fraction away from being feminine.

But there was nothing feminine about Alexis Tsaliki. He was the most rampantly masculine man she'd ever met in her life and sitting in this booth with him, the full weight of his attention on her, she fully understood why he had such a high success rate with the ladies. He didn't need his wealth to attract them. With his classically chiselled face complete with high cheekbones and strong nose, and bronzed skin the sun adored soaking itself into, all enhanced rather than disguised by his trimmed dark goatee beard, the man was sex on legs.

'So in reality, it isn't a truce you want—in any case, there has been an unspoken truce between us since I replaced my father at the top and the Antoniadis board forced your father to resign—you want my help to stop Antoniadis Shipping from going bust.'

'Do you think you could?'

'I'm sure I could.' His gorgeous blue-grey eyes glimmered. 'The question is, what's in it for me? Since I've taken control of the business, the rot has stopped. Our share price is rising. Any contracts lost will be either replaced or regained.'

'That could take years.'

'I can play the long game.'

Now Lydia was the one to bring her face close to his. 'The question, though, is can Tsaliki Shipping afford for you to play the long game?'

Their gazes held, challenge firing from both. And then the smile that had been tugging at Alexis's divine lips pulled into a full-blown grin that filled her chest with an inexplicable warmth. 'Do you drink tequila?'

'Only if it's the good stuff.'

His grin widened. The warmth in her chest spread.

'Lydia?' It was her mother's voice, pulling her out of the memory she'd fallen into.

'I'm here,' she called back, wiping away tears she hadn't felt fall.

Her mother emerged through the trees. 'What are

you…?' She saw the redness of her daughter's eyes and pulled her into an embrace. 'We'll survive, *baba*. You'll see. So long as we all stick together, we can survive this and start again and come back stronger.' She stepped back and cupped Lydia's cheeks. 'Now dry your eyes—those vile Tsaliki people are on the island and I need you by my side to face them because God knows your father and brother are in no state to deal with them.'

'Thanasis has fallen in love with her, hasn't he?' Lydia sniffed.

Her mother's lips thinned. 'He thinks he has, yes, but that kind of witchcraft is fleeting.'

She hesitated to ask, already guessing the answer. 'Witchcraft?'

'How else could Lucie have tricked him into forgetting that she's a viper like the rest of them?'

'So we are all in agreement, then,' Alexis stated, eyeballing every person around the dining table with the exception of Lydia, who he skimmed past. He'd sent her a message saying to meet him on the beach at midnight. Until that hour struck he could not allow himself to think of the news she'd thrown at him or allow himself to think about her. 'We all keep our mouths shut.' At this, he gave his sister an extra-hard stare.

Athena gave him her most innocent look.

Of all his many siblings, Athena was the one Alexis had always struggled the most to like, and it had nothing to do with her being the only female sibling. He loved her and would protect her with his life, but she had a bitchy streak that rivalled their stepmother's, and it was Athena who was responsible for knocking the first domino that had led to their stepsister, the bride, running away. For all his cool words to the Antoniadises, Alexis did not have confidence that the Tsalikis could get through this unscathed, not after everything that had already happened. They were all at the precipice, closer to falling into the abyss than they'd ever been, and it was down to him to make sure they all knew and understood what was at stake.

'I mean it,' he said grimly, addressing Athena directly. 'You do not breathe a word of what's happened here. We can only hope that Lucie doesn't go running to the press—'

'She won't,' a dull-eyed Thanasis interjected.

'I agree that it's unlikely.' His stepsister had a visceral hatred of the press. 'And so we all play the long game.' For a moment he lost his train of thought, his words pulling him back three months. He blinked the memory away and studiously avoided seeking out the hazel eyes of the woman he'd once delivered those same words to. 'We play the long game,' he reiterated, 'and ride it out. We say nothing because anything we do say can be contradicted if—and I know it's an unlikely if—Lucie speaks out or releases a statement.'

Addressing Athena directly again, he spoke slowly and elucidated every word. 'If you speak about this to anyone outside these walls, I will see that you're cut off. That goes for all of you.'

Outrage came from half a dozen voices, including his

usually gregarious father who, like Petros Antoniadis, had spent the entire meeting mute. Both family patriarchs had retreated into themselves.

Alexis slammed his fist on the table. 'Enough! Athena is lucky that she's still allowed to call herself a Tsaliki. The wedding might be off but the peace brokered between myself and Thanasis isn't.' He put a finger lightly to the cut on his lip caused by Thanasis's fist. 'The only thing that's over is the war between our two families.'

Lydia sensed movement and had just enough time to brace herself before the figure appeared from the shadows. It had been the longest day of her life and was only going to get longer. Everything she'd had to cope with so far would be a piece of cake compared to what was coming for her now.

The hulking figure sank heavily onto the sand beside her.

For the longest time, neither of them spoke. The air, though, spoke with a tension thick enough to slice with a spoon.

'So we're going to be parents,' he eventually said.

'Yes.'

'And you want to marry me.'

'No.'

He grunted a laugh. 'I would never allow a child of mine to suffer and that includes suffering with poverty. You don't need me to marry you for that—I will give you everything you need and more.'

Lydia lifted her gaze to the stars, She thought the night sky was why she loved Sephone so much. Here, the lack of light pollutants made the stars shine brighter and in millions times greater numbers than anywhere else on earth. Anywhere that she'd ever been in any case, and it broke her heart for all her family that Thanasis would probably have to sell it.

'I'm sorry, Alexis,' she said in as steady a voice as she could manage, 'but I need the security of marriage.'

'You don't,' he contradicted firmly.

'My parents are going to disown me. They will never accept a grandchild who's half Tsaliki and they will never forgive me for...for...' She swallowed to force her next words out. 'For sleeping with you.'

And they had slept. It hadn't just been all sex. For two beautiful nights they'd turned their phones off and hidden from the world in his bedroom. They'd talked and talked about anything and everything that wasn't their families, watched old films and fallen asleep entwined in each other's arms. It had been the most magical time of her life.

'They won't disown you,' he said tightly. 'You Antoniadises are a close-knit bunch.'

'My mother will see it as a betrayal. She hates you more than my father does. I think he only ever hated your father, but my mother hates all of you and when she finds out she will hate me too.'

'She loves you.'

'That won't stop her from hating me. She didn't speak to her sister for seven years because she found out my aunt had gone to a party hosted by the school bully who'd made Mum's life a misery. She holds onto her grudges and does not forgive. I need security for me and the baby, and I need it now. I need to wake up and know that no matter what happens, we'll have a roof over our heads and food in our bellies.'

'I'll buy you a house and pay for its upkeep.'

'And what if you decide to take it away from me or stop paying the bills towards it? I'd be at your mercy and I can't do that any more. It's only since I found out I'm pregnant that I see how entirely at my family's mercy I am. I live in a cottage on the grounds but it's not mine, it's theirs. I make a living selling my designs to clothing and fabric companies but I've not built a big enough name to sustain myself—I suppose I never really needed to as the company shares my parents assigned me when I was born have always given me a decent income, but that's going to be ripped away with everything else. I've always had a mental safety net around me and it's all being ripped away and when my parents learn about the baby they will cut me off and I'll be on my own and I will have nothing. Being on my own frightens me enough but being on my own with a baby to feed terrifies me.

'As your wife, you won't be able to just throw me out and leave me with nothing. I'll sign whatever prenuptial agreement you want—marriage won't cost you anything more than it would if you were to just buy me a house.'

In the silence that followed, the beats of Lydia's

heavy heart seemed to speed up to a burr, its weight compressing her stomach.

This was a conversation she'd never wanted to have. Never expected to have. The marriage between her brother and Lucie Burton was supposed to save their business and fortune, and even if her parents turned their backs on her, Thanasis never would. She'd longed to confide in him but he'd been under so much stress trying to save the business and convincing the world that his fake engagement was true love that she'd not wanted to add to his burden, not until after the wedding.

All her plans had been ripped away in the same way her future was being, and the only thing that mattered, the only thing she could allow to matter, was the tiny life nestled in her womb.

'Say I go along with this mad idea,' the father of her tiny life said slowly. 'What's in it for me?'

Lydia closed her eyes at the virtual repeat of words spoken all those months ago. 'You'll be able to watch our child grow up and be as involved…or not…as you wish.' She forced a smile to her face so the movements would inject lightness into her voice to deliver what she knew would be the greatest selling point to him. 'And just think what an excellent excuse having a wife in the background of your life will give you when your lovers become too demanding of your time. I won't make any demands on you or your time—you'll be able to live your life exactly as you've always lived it. I won't even have to live with you. I'll be your wife in name only.'

Alexis Tsaliki was a serial seducer. Flirting came as

naturally to him as breathing. He didn't even have to try. All he had to do was fix those hypnotic blue-grey eyes on a woman and she was his. Lydia should know. That was how it had been for her. She hadn't gone to that nightclub with the intention to seduce or be seduced—talking to him had been the only thing on her mind—but Alexis had a power about him that turned a level-headed adult female into a creature held hostage by its own desires. She couldn't even blame it on the champagne or tequila. He'd made her heart beat faster from the moment he'd slid into the booth beside her. By the time he'd invited her back to his apartment her body had become such a hot mess of desire for him that if he'd suggested going outside for a quick knee-trembler instead, she'd have given the same answer.

Until she'd met Alexis, she'd never had a fling; never even considered one. In her twenty-seven years she'd had two lovers, both long-term, serious relationships with serious, arty men who wouldn't be seen dead in a boardroom or in a suit. Neither had come within a fraction of thrilling her or rousing the woman in her as Alexis had done.

A man like Alexis Tsaliki was untameable. Only a fool would let themselves believe otherwise and Lydia was no fool. She'd gone to his apartment with her eyes wide open—his sexploits were legendary in Greek society—and what had been a spontaneous magically, passionately glorious one-off for her was just a regular weekend of fun to him. That was why when she'd woken late on the Sunday morning racked with a tsunami of emotions she'd never felt before, including guilt for such a heinous betrayal to her family, she'd made sure to be the one to say their weekend together had been a one-off that no one could ever know about.

While he'd carried on with his life, no doubt not giving her even a passing thought, she'd thought about him practically every second of every minute of every day.

Her weekend with Alexis had been the best worst mistake of her life.

'Okay,' he eventually said in that same slow, thoughtful voice. 'I'll do it.'

Her heart jumped into her throat. 'You'll marry me?'

She hadn't expected it to be that easy. That quick.

'Yes.' She felt his stare land on her skin. 'But I have conditions.'

'Anything.' This was no time for pride. Her family could be bankrupt in weeks and within that timeframe there was a very good chance the pregnancy would start showing. She couldn't keep this a secret much longer. She needed to sort her and her baby's future out now.

'If I'm going to marry you then it's on condition that it's a real marriage.'

CHAPTER THREE

ALEXIS FELT AS well as saw the woman sitting on the sand beside him with her arms hugging her knees freeze.

When she responded, it was in a higher voice than the even, reasonable tone she'd carried the conversation with up to that point. 'It isn't necessary to have a real marriage.'

'It is for me.'

'Why?'

'A number of reasons. One—because marriage is not a game to be played, whether it's to gain yourself an advantage or for any other reason. Two—because I will not have the humiliation of the world believing my wife despises me enough that she won't share my bed, and three—because a real marriage between you and me might just do the job Thanasis and Lucie's marriage was supposed to do.'

'Do you seriously think anyone will be fooled by that trick a second time?'

He shrugged. 'Our baby will be all the proof we need.'

'Not neces…'

'That's my condition. A real marriage. Husband, wife, one bed, till death us do part. Take it or leave it.'

A tremor came into her voice. 'When you say one bed…'

'Yes. Sex.' He allowed himself a half-smile, allowed a partial memory of their nights together to infiltrate his mind, of Lydia on top of him, throwing her head back in rapture as she'd climaxed with such force her spasming contractions had pulled him over the edge too. With a snapped blink, he shuttered the vivid memory away and added, 'I figure you should be allowed some enjoyment within it.'

She spluttered with outrage then shook her head vigorously. 'No sex.'

'Then no deal.'

'You don't need to have…'

'You said you'd agree to anything, and that's my price. If I'm going to commit to you and our baby then you can damned well commit to me too. A real marriage, Lydia. All or nothing. Say yes and I will fly you to Agon tomorrow and marry you there on Sunday. In less than forty-eight hours you will be my wife. Say no and take your chances that your worst fears won't be proved right.'

He could feel her turmoil like a wave of tension vibrating off her skin.

Until the night she'd come to his nightclub—and only a select few of his inner circle knew he owned the nightclub as part of his vast portfolio of personal investments—Lydia had been a face he'd known only as a member of the Antoniadis family. A pretty face for sure, but there were plenty of pretty faces in his world and as her pretty face was one he associated with poisonous scorpions, not one he'd had any wish to know.

That she'd appeared in his club seeking him out hadn't been in question, and he'd joined her in her booth fully expecting to be only moments away from calling security to eject her from his premises.

There were many things he hadn't expected when he took that seat beside her: not her reasons for seeking him out, not the open, warm curiosity in her hazel eyes, not the witty playfulness, and definitely not the click of attraction that had sprung almost immediately between them.

He'd invited her to his apartment knowing she would say yes and knowing it had nothing to do with her request for his help, which had been barely spoken about as they'd shared the best part of a bottle of tequila between them and a mountain of chips, and exchanged increasingly more outrageous stories about mutual acquaintances that had them both roaring with laughter. By the time he'd issued his invitation, her legs had been draped over his lap, their hands had been clasped tightly together and their eyes might as well have been glued together because they'd both stopped seeing anyone else.

If one of them had carried a condom, he'd have taken her…or she'd have taken him…before his driver had left the underground car park. *Theos*, he could still remember the thrill of electricity that had coursed through him at the first touch of her tongue against his, still remember the pulsation the first time her fingers had wrapped around his erection, still remember the sound of her first climax cried into his mouth as they'd pleasured each other with their hands.

He'd never known a night like it, a hedonistic, instinctive compatibility that had blown his mind and, instead of sating him, had kept him wanting more; kept them both wanting more. One night had rolled into day and then into another night, time managing to stand still and yet pass in the blink of an eye.

Scorpions had bite but, as he'd discovered that weekend, they tasted divine.

It was on the Sunday that Lydia had unleashed the sting in her tail.

She'd woken him with a quick shake of his shoulder. He'd opened his eyes to find her dressed and the bedroom bathed in daylight.

'I have to go.'

He'd thrown the sheets off to reveal an erection that no man should have been able to produce after the two nights they'd shared. 'Sure about that?'

She'd darted her gaze away. 'Sorry. Things to do.'

He'd sat up and cupped her face before kissing her deeply and then murmuring, 'Dinner tonight?'

She'd pulled away from him and climbed off the bed. Her blonde hair had been all mussed from their lovemaking, her face bare, not a scrap of makeup. He'd never seen a sight so beautiful.

'I can't.'

'Tomorrow night?'

She'd raised her gaze to the ceiling. 'Alexis...what we've shared has been...great, but we can't see each other again.'

His limbs still heavy from all their incredible lovemaking, his loins primed and ready for more, he'd pulled a face. 'Why not?'

Her stare had whipped to him. All the passion and light that had shone from the beautiful hazel eyes had gone. Now all that had rung out from them had been incredulity. 'You have to ask? Seeing each other again is out of the question.'

'If you're worried about our families then don't be—they don't need to know.'

'They must *never* know,' she'd said with such vehemence his hackles had risen. 'No one can ever know and we both need to forget that anything happened.'

It had been his turn to be incredulous. 'How the hell am I supposed to do that?'

'By not thinking about it and not speaking about it. You can't tell anyone, no one, not even your confessor.'

'People saw you leaving the club with me. If you know a way to wipe their memories then I'm all ears.'

'People saw you leaving with one of your interchangeable blondes. No one there would have recognised me—I'm a jeans and baggy T-shirt and ponytail girl, not a mini-dress girl, and the people who know me are more house-party people than nightclub people.'

He'd stared at her with narrowed eyes, a scenario playing out in his head that had driven out the last of the languid contentment and filled his mouth with a bitter taste. 'Did you dress up like that deliberately to seduce me?'

'No! I dressed like that to blend in and capture your attention so we could talk. I didn't think for a minute that *this* was going to happen.' She'd said *this* as if it were a dirty word.

'By *this* do you mean spending the weekend with me, screwing each other's brains out?'

Colour had slashed her cheeks but she hadn't dropped her stare. 'I don't know what you're talking about. I had a few drinks too many at a party on Friday night and slept on my friend's sofa and ended up staying the weekend, and you spent the weekend with one of your legions of lovers.'

'Oh, did I?' he'd queried silkily. Dangerously.

She'd stood tall; determined and unwavering. 'Yes, you did.'

Loathing that had morphed from nothing had crackled between them until Alexis had lain himself back down, hooked an arm over the top of his head and casually said, 'You can see yourself out. If any of the staff see you, introduce yourself by any name you like— you're as interchangeable as all the others who've done the walk of shame from here.'

She'd looked him over one more time, her face now contorted with hatred, and walked out without another word.

Only when she'd closed the door behind her had

he clenched his jaw and punched his fist down on the mattress.

The irony that three months later the only woman to have ever walked out on him would be so desperate for help that she wanted marriage should be something to savour, and he had no doubt that when she capitulated to his demands he *would* savour it.

'I need to get back to the yacht, so it's make your mind up time,' he said roughly when she still hadn't answered. 'Do I make arrangements to fly us to Agon tomorrow or do I get one of my people on the job of buying a house for you to live in?'

'You've thrown me,' she whispered.

'I was thrown earlier when a not particularly memorable one-weekend stand told me I'd got her pregnant and wanted me to marry her, so consider us even.'

The brightness of the stars highlighted her features and allowed him to see the flinch his deliberate barb had induced.

Theos, if only that barb had been the truth...

'I'm out of here,' he said, hauling himself up. 'I'll be in touch. Good luck dealing with the fallout with your family.'

He'd taken four steps when she called, 'Okay, I'll do it.'

He stopped walking. 'Do what?'

'Have a real marriage with you.'

He turned around. She was on her feet, gripping her arms. 'But I have conditions too.'

'You're not in a position to make conditions.'

'The wedding has to be secret—I want to hold off telling anyone for as long as possible. My family are under a great deal of stress…'

'As are mine.'

'I appreciate that but my family is very different from yours and my parents are on the brink of losing everything. I don't want to add to the enormous stress they're under until I absolutely have to because I think you and me might be the thing that tips them over the edge. You have no reason to feel sympathy for them but they're my parents and I love them.'

'You cannot protect them for ever,' he pointed out, and allowed his gaze to do what he'd fought it from doing since he'd ridden the jet ski onto the beach, and take in every inch of her. Only now, under the full moon, could he see the subtle changes to her figure that only someone who'd been intimate with her and had committed every inch of her flesh to memory would notice: the pushing of her stomach against the three-quarter-length ripped jeans, the new fullness of breasts that had been perfection itself beneath the baggy white top. Now, she would struggle to squeeze herself into the silver dress that had done its job of capturing his attention so spectacularly well it should win its own special award. 'You will be showing soon.'

The jutting of her chin only proved that she felt every inch of his stare. 'I know.'

'And it's not in my interests to keep it secret.'

'A month. That's all I'm asking for. A month.'

'I will give you a week.'

'But...'

'A week or nothing.' He made to walk away.

'Fine,' she snapped. 'A week. But a week from the wedding.'

'Deal.' He gave a mocking smile. 'Our first compromise.'

'Hardly a compromise.'

'You should be more grateful—I didn't need to compromise. I don't need to compromise on anything. That we're standing here even discussing this is entirely for your benefit.'

'No, for our *baby's* benefit.'

'Once you know me better you will know our baby's security was never in doubt.'

'If it wasn't for our baby I wouldn't want to know you at all.'

'But you, my angel from Hades, do know me, and *intimately*.' He had the satisfaction of seeing her beautiful face contort at the reminder. 'Any other conditions?'

'No.'

'No demands that I be faithful?' he said with another mocking smile.

Her loathing was so visible he swore he could taste it. 'I wouldn't waste my breath.'

He laughed. 'In that case, I believe we have a deal.'

'Whoopee,' she said flatly.

'It is usually customary that a deal be sealed with a handshake, but in these circumstances I believe a kiss would be more appropriate.'

She shook her head with a sneering laugh and took a small step back.

'I'm serious, Lydia. We seal the deal and you prove your commitment to us having a real marriage with a kiss, otherwise the deal is non-binding and you have no guarantee I will sign my name on any wedding certificate.'

Her eyes were ablaze with fury. 'You're enjoying this, aren't you? Humiliating me.'

'Very much so, but not as much as I'm going to enjoy feeling your delectable mouth against mine again, so come here and seal the deal.' He pressed a finger to the cut her brother's fist had made on his mouth. 'You can start by kissing this better.'

Lydia tried to hold her ground but the expression on Alexis's face was uncompromising.

This was payback. She knew it. He knew it. Payback for her doing the unthinkable and being the one to walk out on the great Alexis Tsaliki when his ego dictated that he play his lovers like a puppeteer until he bored of them.

If he had any idea that dragging herself out of his bed had been the hardest thing she'd ever had to do... His ego would explode.

She was glad, now, that their circumstances had forced her to go against all her instincts and walk away, because she would have given anything to stay in his bed; given anything to have kissed him back and said yes to dinner with him.

She'd never dreamed making love could feel like

that. Be like that. Passionate. Tender. Thrilling. Fun. She'd never believed, either, that she could be like that with someone. Alexis hadn't just stripped her clothes from her but stripped her bare too. He'd peeled away all her layers to reveal the essence of who she was as a woman, a woman who for one gloriously hedonistic weekend had lived only for him. She would love to believe the alcohol they'd consumed and the fact that even talking civilly to each other was a massive taboo had played their part in heightening everything, and maybe they had, to start with, but they hadn't touched a drop of alcohol once at his apartment and she'd been stone-cold sober when she'd had to physically wrench herself away from him...

During their weekend together, she hadn't once forgotten that it was her enemy's bed she'd willingly climbed into, but she had forgotten what kind of man her enemy was. A ruthless man. A man who'd wrested control of his own father's company against his father's wishes and, as she'd learned that day, had had no compunction about serving his stepsister to Lydia's brother on a platter built on a lie.

He was also a man for whom commitment was a dirty word, and why would it not be when he had the looks that would make any passing human take a second look? Combine that with his wealth and you had a man who could have anyone he pleased, and frequently did. If their families' entwined poisonous histories hadn't forced Lydia to drag herself out of his bed and walk away, the most she could have looked forward to would have been a couple of dates before being unceremoniously dumped for the next woman to catch his forever roving eye.

Regardless of their poisonous family histories, she would never have been that woman. Lydia's pride and self-respect were the only things she'd ever earned on her own and she would not compromise them for anyone, not even Mr Sex on Legs.

She'd walked away and so bruised his overinflated ego, and now he was snatching at the opportunity their carelessness—and as hard as she tried, she couldn't pinpoint when, exactly, throughout that long, glorious weekend the passion had made them *that* careless—had provided to make her pay.

He beckoned her with his finger.

This was her last chance. Prove her commitment or he would walk.

But to prove her commitment she had to walk to him. She wouldn't have been surprised if he'd clicked his fingers to lay a path of hot coals for her to tread to reach him.

Heart racing, pulses jumping, she lifted her chin and took the five steps needed to reach him.

His lips tugged into a knowing smile. 'Here first,' he said, lowering his face to nearer her level and lightly tapping the only thing close to a blemish on his face. Not liking the constriction in her chest to be forced to look at that blemish and to remember the blood that had poured from it, she gritted her teeth, and rose onto her toes.

Holding her breath, she pressed her lips swiftly to the side of Alexis's mouth where the cut lay, then stepped back before her lips had the time to register any connection between them.

It didn't stop her heart racing even harder and faster.

His eyes gleamed as he placed his finger to the centre of his mouth. 'And now here.'

She clenched her jaw to rise back onto her toes and press an even more fleeting kiss to the lips that had kissed her in places she hadn't even known were places. Before she could dart back out of his reach and thank years of yoga and Pilates for giving her a core that could lift itself to kiss a man over a foot taller than herself without having to lay a finger on him for support, an arm hooked around her back and pulled her flush to him.

'You call that a kiss?' he whispered huskily. His other hand clasped the back of her head and gently tugged her back, forcing her to meet head-on the blue-grey eyes that had haunted her waking and sleeping dreams for three months. 'Let me show you the kind of kiss I was thinking of...'

His mouth closed in on hers and with her heart now a thrumming burr and her mouth filled with a moisture that had come from nowhere, Lydia closed her eyes. Before she could clench her hands into fists or do any of the other things necessary to keep her senses dulled, there was a gentle, featherlight pressure on her lips and a scent filled her nostrils that made every cell in her body cry.

Determined not to react, she held herself like a statue. Of all the things that had made her recoil from committing to a proper marriage, the strongest had been Alexis's devastating physical effect on her. So powerful had it been that dragging herself out of his bed had been the hardest thing she'd had to do in the whole of her life. She could not imagine what a month of waking in his arms would do to her, never mind a lifetime. Telling herself that this was all a power play and that she'd probably only share his bed for an extremely limited time before he bored of toying with her and bored of *her*—a goldfish had a greater attention span than Alexis Tsaliki had with women—didn't make her feel any better. Somehow it made her feel worse.

She had no choice. Alexis held all the cards and when you made a deal with the devil you had to pay the price. But that didn't mean you had to pay a cent more than he demanded, and if she could make it to the point where he discarded her with her pride and self-respect intact, then she...

The distraction of her thoughts evaporated under the heat of the slow, seductive movements of his mouth and the gentle massaging of his fingers to the back of her head.

With skilful mastery, he coaxed her lips apart and slowly slid his tongue into her mouth.

Her entire system short-circuited.

She swayed, suddenly filled with the dark, exotic taste that had been part of the whole magical Alexis Tsaliki package, and a flame of raw desire pulsed from the spot between her legs and darted straight into her veins, weakening her legs.

The probing of his tongue deepened, the fingers clasping her head moving up to the band holding her hair in place and then gently sliding it down to the tips and flicking it away. Her hair tumbled down at the same moment her throat betrayed her with a treacherous moan and suddenly Lydia was gripping his strong shoulders and moulding herself to the hardness of his chest, not just responding to the demands of his mouth and tongue but making demands of her own.

With his fingers now threading through the strands of her hair, his other hand clasped her bottom, holding it possessively, the fusion of their bodies as tight as that of their mouths. Arms now wrapped around his neck, she kissed him as if she'd been waiting her whole life for this moment, and when she felt the hard ridge of his arousal against her abdomen she moved restlessly against it, rising onto the tips of her toes in a desperate effort to lift her pelvis closer.

His hand crept up, beneath her cotton top, the heat of his skin burning into her flesh, moving higher to the clasp of her bra. With a practised flick of his fingers and wrist, he undid the clasp, making her a hundred times more aware of the weight of her own breasts crying out for his touch, and when his fingers skimmed her ribcage and then covered one, she cried into his mouth and scraped her nails down the nape of his neck to dip beneath the collar of his polo shirt, a fever inside her, needing to touch him as much as she needed to be touched...

With no warning and no ceremony, he dropped his hands and pulled away from her, mouth and body.

'Wha...?' She tried to snatch a breath, her dazed, unthinking word fading into nothing.

Muscular arms now folded across his broad chest, his face lowered to hers. The lips that had just kissed her senseless smiled cruelly. 'That, my angel from Hades, was a much better effort. Our deal is now sealed. Can you get yourself to Kos tomorrow?'

She nodded dumbly. She could barely stand never mind speak, had to ground her feet in the sand to stop her legs from giving out on her.

'Good. My plane will leave for Agon at four p.m. If you're not there then I will assume you have changed your mind and our deal will be terminated.'

With those parting words, he turned his back and walked away. Lydia was still fighting to find breath when he was swallowed by the darkness.

CHAPTER FOUR

ALEXIS TAPPED HIS long fingers on the armrest and gazed out at the seemingly endless stretch of tarmac. Five minutes until take-off and no sign of Lydia.

He caught the questioning eye of his senior cabin crew member and shook his head. He'd told Lydia four p.m. and he would give her until the clock turned the hour. But not a minute more.

He took a long breath and stretched his legs out. His chest had been tight since he'd got out of bed. He hadn't slept a wink. Too much going on in his head. By rights, he should be hunting down Lucie and gathering all the board members together to drive forward a solid plan to save Tsaliki Shipping from the fate that was coming for Antoniadis Shipping. If Tsaliki Shipping went down then his personal wealth would be safe. Alexis had diversified over the years, building himself a portfolio of assets that had made him a billionaire in his own right before he'd reached thirty. Ultimately, his family would be safe too because he would never let them suffer poverty.

Four minutes.

Alexis had never wanted to take control of his father's company. In truth, he'd never had much interest in the business, but he was the oldest son and it had been expected by his father and, growing up, he'd hero-worshipped the man. It wasn't until he'd become an adult himself that he'd finally admitted to himself that his father's feet were made of clay, and it wasn't until his siblings came of age one by one that he realised none of them had the ability to step into their father's clay business shoes. They were all spoilt; a bunch of useless, work-shy wastrels living off daddy's largesse. Constantine at least tried, but he had no business acumen and zero judgement.

Three minutes.

If Alexis did manage to save Tsaliki Shipping then a hard conversation would need to be had because once all this was done with, he wanted out. So yes, he should be concentrating on the damned business he didn't even want to run and finding a way to save it from a fate that would leave his entire family dependent on *his* largesse, not making covert plans to marry the one woman in the world who despised him. Make that two women. He didn't imagine Lucie's opinion of him was particularly high at that moment, but Lucie wasn't blood and had been too young when her mother had married his father for Alexis to take any interest in her. And she wasn't pregnant with his child.

Theos, he was going to be a father. Since Lydia had bamboozled him with the news, it had sat in him like an extra beat in his heart. Maybe at some point soon he'd have the time to actually think about what that meant. But not yet. Not when he had so much else to think about and contend with.

Two minutes.

He took another deep breath and gave another shake of his head to the stewardess.

Lydia wasn't coming but he would still let the clock count down.

He closed his eyes briefly and allowed himself the luxury of remembering how she'd come apart at the seams on the beach. Only ruthless determination had allowed him to hold onto his own control. He'd had a point to make to them both and he'd damned well made it.

One minute.

He straightened, swallowed the constriction in his throat and opened his mouth to instruct the crew...and then he saw it, a blur in the corner of his eye. A scooter carrying two people speeding towards his plane.

It stopped at the steps that were twenty seconds away from being removed and the passenger jumped off, tugged off her helmet, handed it to the rider and with a quick wave of goodbye raced up the metal steps clutching a small black handbag and virtually threw herself through the door.

Alexis looked at his watch and then looked her up and down. Dressed in tight black trousers, black ankle books and a loose black sheer blouse, all Lydia needed was a black veil and she'd fit in perfectly as chief mourner at a funeral. He was quite sure she'd chosen the outfit for that specific effect and was equally sure, judging by the faint sheen of perspiration on her face and the way her fringe was sticking to her forehead, that she must be roasting in it.

'You look...hot.' In more ways than one, because he was quite sure too that she was oblivious to the fact that the sunlight pouring through the plane's windows had made her blouse transparent and that he could see the pattern of her black lace bra beneath it.

The delectably plump lips tightened, defiance shining from her hazel eyes even as colour rose on her cheeks. 'And you look smug.'

He couldn't argue with that. She was there, throwing herself at his mercy.

Sinking onto the seat across from his, she strapped herself in, aimed the air-conditioning console above her head to her face, and turned her gaze out of the window. 'Are we going or what?'

Or what...?

Throw Lydia to her fate or save her?

Alexis caught the eye of the senior stewardess and nodded.

Minutes later they were in the air.

The skies were so clear and the sun so bright that even at over thirty thousand feet, Lydia could see the white dots of yachts in the blue sea far below them. She wondered if any of those dots were guests at the wedding that had never taken place.

'Did you get cold feet?'

She pulled in a breath before casting a brief glance at the man sitting opposite her whose kisses she could still taste and whose hand she could still feel on the naked skin of her back. It was the first time he'd spoken since they'd taken off.

It wasn't fair that he should look all fresh and rugged and gorgeous while a night of no sleep whatsoever, along with choosing the most impractical clothes to race across Kos in a heatwave with, had left her looking like death warmed up. She wished she could blame her lack of sleep on her family's dire predicament messing with her head but it was all Alexis and the mortifying way she'd melted for him messing with her body and her mind, and it was Alexis's fault, too, that she'd chosen to dress all in black. She'd wanted to send him a message but all she'd done was make herself hot and bothered in the only black clothing she'd packed for Sephone, and while the plane's excellent air conditioning was cooling her skin, it was having no effect whatsoever on her core temperature, and that was all Alexis's fault too.

She hated that he'd spent the short time they'd been in the air concentrating on his laptop as if she weren't right there with him, as if he felt *nothing* to have her right there with him. She hated too that the powerful awareness inside her for him was a living entity she had no control over whereas he could turn any attraction on and off like a tap.

For heaven's sake, he was wearing a white shirt and suit trousers, clothing that had always turned her off men, what with it being the attire her father and brother lived in, and he was *still* sex on legs.

'No,' she answered shortly. Not cold feet in the sense that she'd come close to backing out. Backing out was not an option. The only person capable of saving her family was her brother, and he was falling apart. Marrying Alexis would give Lydia the security she needed for her and her baby and maybe, in time, *she* would have the means to help her family. It made her heart clench to imagine them rejecting that help. Rejecting her. Rejecting her baby.

'Ah, you just thought you'd keep me on my toes by waiting until the last second to arrive, then.'

'I don't know where you get your ego from but not everything is about you. There was an engine problem with the yacht so we left Sephone later than planned.' Beneath the coolness of her tone, Lydia could still feel the panic that had clawed at her as she'd watched the hours slip by. Thank God for her old friend Maya, who'd made her home on Kos and who'd dropped everything to meet Lydia at the harbour and speed her to the airport, no questions asked.

'What excuse did you come up with to justify not returning to Athens with them?'

'I told them I was going to stay with one of my English friends to get away from everything.'

'You told them you were taking a trip to England and didn't pack any luggage?'

Gritting her teeth at his mocking scepticism, her reply was a short, 'I had to leave it at the harbour.'

As much as she'd despaired at leaving her luggage behind—Maya had promised to go back for it and walk it to her apartment for safekeeping—it was impossible to carry suitcases on a scooter. Being late for the flight would have caused a million times more despair. If she'd arrived one minute later, the door into Alexis's private plane would have been closed to her. 'I'll need to go shopping when we get to Agon.'

'I'm afraid that isn't possible. Agon's trading laws forbid retailers to open after five at weekends.'

'Even for hotel boutiques?'

'We're not stopping in a hotel.'

Great. So she was going to be stuck in this awful outfit for the foreseeable future. When life threw crap at you, it *really* threw it at you. 'Fine. I'll marry you in this outfit, then. At least it'll be fitting.'

He laughed softly. 'From your perspective, certainly. Did your family believe your excuse?'

'They had no reason not to—they're used to me flying off to stay with friends.'

'That's good to know.'

There was something in his tone that made her turn her stare to him. 'Why?'

Those gorgeous blue-grey eyes bored into her. 'It's good to know the excuses your wife will use when she lies to you.'

She held his stare with all the contempt she could muster. 'When people lie it's either to stop themselves getting into trouble or to spare the other's feelings. Unless you're planning to beat me to keep me in line, which I don't think even *you* would do, I have no need to lie to you, because I couldn't care less about your feelings.'

There was the slightest flicker in his eye before he gave a half-smile. 'Then I look forward to the day I catch you in a lie.'

And with those unsettling, enigmatic words, he dropped his stare back to his laptop and immersed himself back in his work.

It was movement that woke her. Disorientated, Lydia had to blink a number of times before she remembered where she was. Flying to Agon with Alexis Tsaliki to marry him...

Where was he?

Rubbing the sleep out of her eyes—it must have claimed her quickly as she didn't remember her eyes getting heavy—she looked at her watch. Only forty minutes in the air. She could only have been asleep for minutes.

She straightened, her heart catching in her throat before her eyes registered the figure further down the cabin, in the dining area.

His back to her, Alexis had changed out of his trousers into a pair of faded jeans that perfectly accentuated his perfect buttocks and snake hips, and was leaning over, pulling something out of a carry-on bag, the muscles of his bronzed naked back rippling with the movement.

Her caught heart swelled and she gripped hold of her blouse right above the place it beat the hardest.

He straightened and then more muscles rippled and flexed as he lifted his arms and pulled a white T-shirt over his head.

'Enjoying the show?' he asked before he turned around and flattened the T-shirt over his rock-hard abdomen. Eyes gleaming, he strode towards her. 'I would have showered but time ran away from me.'

She wanted to run away from him. Lydia had never gone so fully from dozing to wide awake in such a short space of time.

'I would suggest you change into something more comfortable too, but with your clothing predicament…' Shaking his head with faux regret, he retook his seat and stretched his long legs out, his foot coming to rest right beside hers. Eyes alive with sensuous amusement, he smiled. 'Unless you would like to borrow something of mine?'

Lydia pulled her feet back. 'I'd rather suffer, thank you.'

'Then you will soon get your wish—we'll be landing in a few minutes.'

Stepping out of the plane and onto the private airfield was like stepping into an inferno. From the time it took to walk from the door of the plane to the door of the shining black car waiting for them, a feat that took approximately twenty seconds, Lydia's clothes were clinging to her skin and the hair at the nape of her neck had dampened, which also happened to be Alexis's fault because it had been too dark to find the hairband he'd pulled out on the beach and she didn't have a spare. It was all grossly unfair—she'd seen daisies that would envy his freshness.

Reaching into her handbag, she pulled out her phone. 'Where are we staying?' She would do a quick search to see if there was a hotel with a boutique close by that she could zip into.

'At my villa.'

'I didn't know you had a villa here.'

'I have many properties. This is but one of them.'

'The address?'

He recited it to her. To her immense frustration, it was in an exclusive area with high-end restaurants and boutiques but no hotels.

'We can shop in the morning, before we marry,' he said, reading her thoughts.

'Is it booked?'

'Yes. We marry at the royal chapel at midday.'

It took a moment for that to sink in. 'The royal chapel?' she said in horror. 'Are you being serious? I assumed we were having a civil ceremony?'

'Then you assumed wrong. Prince Talos is an old friend and immensely trustworthy. He's made the arrangements, and is going to act as a witness with his wife. No one will know we've married until we release the news.'

'But a chapel? How am I supposed to make my vows in front of God knowing it's a lie?'

His eyes narrowed a touch before he said in a silkily dangerous voice, 'But it can't be a lie when you're committing to a real marriage with me, until death us do part...unless that in itself is a lie and you're already planning your escape?'

'I don't need to plan anything because if anyone's going to want to escape it, it's *you*.'

The almost imperceptible flicker appeared in his eye. 'And what makes you think that?'

'Because you're a serial seducer who's slept with...' Her stomach turned over. 'I don't want to think about how many women you've been with.'

'Jealous?'

'Don't be ridiculous,' she said before quickly adding, 'It's the reasons behind our marriage that make marrying in a house of God wrong, the vows to love and honour and everything...how can we pledge to love each other when the truth is that we despise each other?' And why did her heart pang to say that?

The strength of his stare in the silence that followed acted like a magnet, forcing her to meet it.

'Why have you never married before?' he surprised her by asking.

'I never wanted to.'

'But if I've been led to believe correctly, you've had two long-term relationships—did you not want to marry those men?'

She turned her stare out of the window. This was her first visit to the island of Agon, a sovereign nation of Greek origin with the same language, currency, myths and legends. The architecture of the pristine town they were driving through reminded her strongly of Crete but with wider roads. She'd holidayed in Crete once, while in her second relationship. The forced proximity she'd assumed they would enjoy together had been the catalyst for their end. She'd been bored out of her mind. 'No.'

'Did you not love them?'

Not enough. 'Of course I loved them.'

'But not enough to marry them,' he observed astutely, correctly reading her thoughts. 'They asked you?'

She sighed. 'Yes.'

'Why say no?'

'That's none of your business.'

'Considering that tomorrow I shall be your husband, it *is* my business.'

'Okay, well I'll answer that if you tell me why you're a serial shagger and commitment-phobe.'

'Hardly a commitment-phobe when I'm marrying you in a matter of hours.'

'Yes, but nothing will change for you. You're not making a commitment to be faithful. You'll still be continuing your serial shagging ways.'

'Your opinion of me never ceases to delight.' Although this was delivered lightly, Lydia detected an edge to his voice, an edge that disappeared when he added, 'But as you're the one who has turned down two marriage proposals, I would say that makes *you* the one afraid of commitment, which is a conversation we shall continue later. We're here.' They'd stopped by the side of the wide road, the driver indicating to turn into a set of high iron gates that were slowly opening. 'For now, I remind you that you have committed yourself to me as my wife, in all ways, and now it is time for you to prove it.'

She whipped her stare back to him. *'How?'*

'Generally people newly in love look at each other with love, so you can start with not looking at me as if you want to bash my brains in when we're in public,' he answered drily.

She jutted her chin mutinously. 'I'm not an actress.'

He gave a nonchalant shrug. 'We made a deal, Lydia. If you're not prepared to stick to it then tell me now and I'll have you driven back to the airport.'

'I'll stick to it.'

'Good, then come here and kiss me.'

'No.'

'Kiss me or go home.'

'I hate you.'

'I know. Now for the last time, come here.'

Jaw clenched, she shuffled across the leather seat to him and twisted to face him properly. The only faint solace she could take at this situation was that this time she was prepared. This time she would keep her composure and wouldn't give an ounce of herself more than necessary.

'How do you want to choreograph it?' she asked tautly. 'Do you want my hands on your shoulders or shall I wrap them around your…?'

Her words were cut off when a large hand cupped

the side of her neck and his mouth swooped onto hers, cutting off her breath with her words as the shock of it raced through her, knotting her stomach and bringing every nerve-ending zinging into tingling life.

With skilled precision, he slid his tongue into her mouth, an arm sliding round her waist, pulling her closer and lighting all those nerve-endings like a match against tissue paper. Lydia, her brain cut off with her breath and her words, melted into him.

Leaning into the kiss, leaning into him, she slid an arm around his neck, and kissed him back, each intimate stroke of their duelling tongues adding to the sizzling excitement building low in her pelvis, would have crawled onto his lap to straddle him if he hadn't pulled away from it.

Ready to cry at the withdrawal of his mouth, she gazed at him in bewilderment, barely able to think under the heavy pounding of her heart, and found herself lost in the blue-grey eyes probing her with a look she couldn't begin to decipher.

After what felt like for ever had passed he rubbed his thumb over her cheek and bent his head for one final, gentle kiss. 'There,' he said softly. 'Now you look like you're in love.'

CHAPTER FIVE

Lydia had no idea how she was able to move from the car into the secluded, whitewashed villa. Alexis's kiss had jellified her legs. That he held her hand jellified the rest of her, and she barely heard the names of the staff she was introduced to. There was a deep, throbbing burn between her thighs and she could only pray she would be able to shower soon to wash away the heat coursing through her veins with cold water. The sun currently melting Agon had nothing on the way Alexis melted her.

She was a tinderbox for his touch, she thought despairingly, despairing even more that a simple holding of hands could feel so thrilling and that she was holding his hand as tightly as he was holding hers. She couldn't even lie to herself that she was holding it so tightly for show like he was. The physical pull Alexis held over her was stronger than her willpower—she had *no* willpower when it came to his touch—and she had to find a way to reverse it, and quickly. Or find a way to dampen it.

So lost in her despairing thoughts was she that when the housekeeper spoke to her, she shook her head to clear her ears because she hadn't heard a word of it. 'I'm sorry, what was that?'

There was avid curiosity on the woman's face…and on the other staff's too, Lydia realised. 'Do you have any dietary requirements?'

'Umm…' Her mind was so all over the place that she had to think. 'No. No. I'll eat anything.'

'Especially chips,' murmured the deep voice belonging to the hand holdings hers so tightly, and a vivid memory flashed in her mind's eye, of Alexis's seductive eyes gleaming while he'd fed chips into her mouth.

Oh, why, why, why did that fun, gorgeous, sexy man she'd felt such a strong connection to in so many ways have to be her family's worst enemy, the serial philanderer Alexis Tsaliki?

Lydia had never understood the war between their families. Okay, she understood the root causes of it—a business partnership between her father and Georgios Tsaliki that had gone wrong—and understood the enmity her father felt towards his old friend and business partner. And she supposed she understood that marital loyalty meant her mother loathed Georgios too, but Lydia had never understood why this loathing extended to every Tsaliki and why it was expected that she despise them too. She'd tried to despise them for her parents' sake but her heart had never been in it. Maybe if she'd gone to the nightclub with her family's loathing for Alexis in her heart, she wouldn't have been so vulnerable to his seductive power…

And she wouldn't have conceived her child. Her innocent, blameless child, the only innocent in this whole sorry mess, and it was thinking of her innocent child that gave her the resolve needed to climb the wide, winding staircase and cross the mezzanine with her child's father knowing that she couldn't back out now just because she melted for him. If protecting her baby meant losing her family to gain a serial seducer as a husband then that was what she would do. What she *was* doing.

The moment he closed the bedroom door she wrenched her hand from his, then found that same hand itching to slap the knowing smile off his face.

Throwing himself onto the sprawling bed piled with pillows, he lay on his back and hooked his arms above his head. It was a pose that brought back memories of his cruel words in the moments before she'd walked out of his bedroom.

'I hope you're not expecting me to share that bed with you tonight,' she said. 'We're not married yet.'

'But, my angel of Hades, we have already sealed the deal on our commitment and, as I told you when we reached our agreement, I will not have the world—and I include my staff in this—believing my wife hates me so much that she won't share my bed.'

'It's bad luck for the bride and groom to sleep together the night before the wedding.'

'I think you'll find it's considered bad luck for the bride and groom to see anything of each other the day *and* night before the wedding,' he told her cheerfully. 'So we've already broken that taboo.'

'You're actively wishing bad luck on us?'

'My father has been married four times and observed all the rituals in all his weddings, and all four ended in divorce.'

'His fourth one hasn't.'

'Oh, yes. I forgot—sorry, must be wishful thinking on my part.'

Lydia had to bite her cheeks to stop herself sniggering at his droll delivery. Rebecca Tsaliki was the stuff of legends, the ordinary Englishwoman who'd captured the heart—or loins—of the macho billionaire philanderer Georgios Tsaliki and not only managed to get herself installed as wife number four but had him so firmly under her manicured thumb that he didn't dare replace her with wife number five, having to content himself with numerous affairs that she didn't bat an eyelash at instead.

Like father like son, and now Lydia was the one with a lifetime of infidelity to look forward to. Somehow she would have to find a way to channel a little of Rebecca Tsaliki's breezy attitude towards it because she couldn't change the son any more than Rebecca had been able to change the father.

She didn't want to change the son, she reminded herself stubbornly. This whole marriage thing was a sham that would be over in all but name as soon as Alexis found himself a new lover because Lydia sure as hell wasn't going to make any demands on him or demand anything from him, and then they could live in perfect marital harmony far apart from each other.

Sitting himself up, he patted the bed. 'From tonight, we sleep together, no arguments.'

'Fine, but no sex until we're married, and no arguments,' she shot back.

His eyes gleamed. 'Wanting to increase the anticipation, are you? I can get on board with that.'

'No, just delaying the inevitable for as long as I can.'

He swung his legs off the bed, laughing. 'I'm going to take a shower. Want to join me?'

She answered with a scowl.

'Sure about that?' Glimmering eyes locked on hers, he strode like a panther towards her.

Although Lydia's every instinct was to hide before she found herself within Alexis touching distance, she folded her arms over her breasts and clenched every cell in her body. 'Very.'

He stopped before her and dipped his mouth to her ear. 'Just imagine it... I would caress soap over every inch of your delectable body, paying special attention to the parts where you're most receptive...and I remember *all* of them...and then I'd lift you against the wall and take you with the water pouring over us...just like I did last time.'

The only part of him touching her was his breath to her ear but the flame that had taken her was strong enough to induce combustion, and it took everything she had not to falter and to find the strength to drag out, 'I'd rather die.'

He laughed softly. 'You forgot to list another reason

people lie...' He lightly covered her breast, feeling its weight and the obvious betraying arousal of her nipple. 'To hide what they're really feeling.' His teeth caught the lobe of her ear and gently pulled before his next murmured words sank straight into her skin. 'And you forget that I know you intimately. I can read your body, Lydia, and it betrays your words.' His tongue licked the tender flesh beneath her lobe as he gently squeezed her breast, sending shivers of arousal through her skin and up her spine. 'Tomorrow you will be mine. *Mine*... For the rest of your life...'

Alexis stood beneath the steaming water and closed his eyes. By rights, he should be exhausted. The hours spent since his talk with Lydia on the beach had been spent fighting fires and getting everything in place for the fires to continue being fought over the coming days. The carefully crafted, ambiguous statement about Thanasis and Lucie's wedding being called off had set off the predictable press feeding frenzy. It didn't help that dozens of the press were already in Greece to cover the wedding.

He wondered if Thanasis now regretted his flat refusal of Alexis's proposal that, to prove they were serious about ending their fathers' war, Alexis marry Lydia. 'Over my dead body,' he'd said, as if he, Alexis, were Caligula reincarnated.

He'd been tempted to casually hand over the lipstick that had fallen out of Lydia's bag when their passion had broken free in the back of his car, and say, 'Can you give this back to your sister for me?' But that would have been his ego talking. For all that Lydia had punched and bruised his ego in the way she'd left him, she didn't deserve the fallout she would have had to deal with.

She would be dealing with the fallout she didn't know he'd protected her from soon enough now. The loathing that had twisted her brother's face at Alexis's suggestion of marriage...

He doubted his own family would be pleased at the turn of events but, as they were currently beholden to his good will, any fallout would be minor ripples compared to the tsunami of opprobrium Lydia could expect from hers. It was one thing to arrange and agree a temporary marriage to cement a truce, quite another to actually be attracted to each other and conceive a child together. He could still feel the hate Lydia's mother had fired at him. There was still a faint mark on his lip where her brother had punched him. Forgiveness did not come easily to those people. It never had. Alexis's father had screwed Lydia's father over decades before, before Lydia was even born, and still the hate burned.

But the attraction burned brighter and she, the woman who'd walked out on him and whose passion had turned to loathing, would be more beholden to him than even his family were.

She was his now. She was carrying his child and, whether her brother liked it or not, tomorrow Lydia would be his wife, and hell would freeze over before he ever let her go.

* * *

Lydia, sitting on the windowsill trying to take in the spectacular view of clear blue seas, turned her head to the opening bathroom door and wasn't quick enough to avert her eyes when Alexis stepped through it with only a towel around his waist. One quick glance was enough to fill her senses with the hard, muscular body she'd spent the last ten minutes studiously refusing to imagine under the shower. Studiously refusing to remember the sculpted perfection of.

Bodies like his should be illegal.

Funny what the memory remembered best though. For Lydia, it hadn't been his sculpted perfection that had stuck so close but the texture of his skin and the taste of his kisses. It was a darkly addictive taste that came from the whole of him, a taste she reacted instinctively and primitively to and that destroyed her willpower with one tiny morsel.

She heard the tread of his footsteps crossing the travertine floor and pressed her hand to her thumping heart.

'Ready for your shower?' he asked in that infuriating cheerful manner he had.

'I've nothing to change into,' she reminded him, refusing to turn her head again.

'I have clothes you can wear.'

'No, thank you,' she said stiffly.

'Afraid that wearing my clothes will feel too much like wearing my skin?'

Unable to think of a retort, she blew out a puff of air.

'We'll be married tomorrow, angel. What is mine becomes yours.'

'No, it doesn't. I already said I'd sign any prenup you demanded.'

'We don't need a prenup.'

That made her turn her head. 'Why not...?' The question had barely left her lips when she made the fatal mistake of dipping her gaze and taking in the unmistakable appendage clearly defined beneath the towel. With a pulse of heat throbbing between her thighs, she shot her gaze back out of the window, but not before she caught the gleam in his eyes.

'You look hot, angel. Sure you don't want to wear my clothes?'

'Oh, shut up,' she muttered. 'And stop calling me "angel".'

'But you are an angel...although I have yet to decide if you come from heaven or only from Hades.'

'Definitely just Hades.'

He laughed lowly, his footsteps treading away. 'What would you prefer I call you? Wife?'

'I'm not your wife.'

'Yet.'

'Why don't you want a prenup?'

'We don't need one. We agreed our marriage would be a commitment for life and I am trusting you to stick to your word.'

'That's a huge risk you're taking.'

'What is life without a little risk?' His voice came closer again. 'Now why don't you take the risk of showering and then change into this shirt? I promise, it will not bite you and I promise you will be a lot more comfortable than you are in those things.'

Wishing she could blame the heat flooding her skin solely on the setting sun's beams penetrating the window, Lydia jumped off the windowsill, snatched the blue garment from Alexis's hand and stomped to the bathroom, all without looking at him. His laughter lingered in her ears long after she'd slammed the bathroom door shut.

Where had this late-onset dose of vanity come from? Lydia wondered with fresh despair. She shouldn't be staring at her reflection wishing for a hairdryer and her makeup bag. She hardly ever wore makeup as it was! And why the hell were her nipples jutting out like that? Alexis would take one look at them and assume she was aroused just from wearing his shirt. Damn him, he'd be right. It really did feel as if she were wearing his skin.

Maybe she should just storm back into the bedroom and push him onto the bed. Get it over with. Use him to get all these hot sticky feelings out of her system and then she'd be able to think more clearly. He wouldn't mind being used in that way. He'd revel in it, his massive ego taking it to mean that she was desperate for him. Damn the bastard, he'd be right, and she would never willingly feed that damned ego or hand any more power to him.

Hanging on the back of the door was a black robe.

She yanked it down and shoved her arms into it, then tied it tightly. It fell to her ankles. After rolling the sleeves, she checked her reflection again and expelled a long breath. Visually, that was much better. Now she was fully covered with an extra layer of protection to stop her treacherous body giving her away.

If only the weight of the robe didn't make her feel as though he were embracing her...

To Lydia's relief, the bedroom had been empty of Alexis. Less of a relief had been the expression on his gorgeous face when she'd appeared on the patio to join him for dinner. Amusement. He'd taken one look at the robe and known exactly why she was wearing it. The worst of it was that he didn't have to say a word, and now she was picking at her food and sweltering under the humid air even more than she'd done earlier when the sun had blazed. She would not give him the satisfaction of asking if they could eat inside where the air-conditioning worked like a dream.

'How many properties do you own?' she asked, just for something to say, something to distract from the heat of the sensuous stare she couldn't stop her eyes from seeking.

'Eight for my personal use. As for my business portfolio...' He shrugged and shook his head. 'Do you want me to include business properties like nightclubs and retail units or just the properties I rent out?'

She blinked. 'You own nightclubs?'

'I own many businesses.'

'I know, but I'd never heard of you owning nightclubs.'

'Most of the businesses I own or invest in are done through a company my name is only attached to if a lot of digging is done.'

'Why the secrecy?'

'I don't need my family knowing my net worth. My siblings have bled my father dry over the years. If I fail to save Tsaliki Shipping then I will have to support them—I *am* supporting them—but they need to learn to fend for themselves.'

She took a moment to digest this. 'Did you know our fathers' rivalry was going to lead to their downfall?'

He speared a lemon potato. 'I saw long ago the way things were headed. The world we live in is very different from the one they lived in when their war started. The bottom line is the bottom line, but investors are no longer so willing to risk reputational damage—it matters much more than it did even a decade ago.'

'That goes for clients too,' she pointed out, thinking of the contracts Tsaliki Shipping had lost since the whole toxicity of the rivalry had been exposed.

He bowed his head in agreement.

'You say about your siblings bleeding your father dry...does that mean you see me as a freeloader too?'

His eyebrows rose in surprise. 'Of course not.'

'I still live with my parents...well, on their estate... and the majority of my income comes from my shares in Antoniadis Shipping.'

'But you still work. You don't rely on your parents' largesse.'

'Of course I do, and from tomorrow I'll be relying on yours, especially when Antoniadis Shipping files for bankruptcy and I lose my income from the shares.'

He fixed her with a stare. 'Have you ever demanded a brand-new penthouse apartment? Or a chalet in Gstaad? Or your own yacht? Or a McLaren fresh off the production line?'

'I wouldn't dream of it, and if I did, I'd be told to buy them myself.'

'And that is my point—my siblings not only dream of those things but see it as their right, and my father never says no. He happily bled money supporting his own lifestyle, Rebecca's, his ex-wives' including my mother's, and all his children.'

'Including Lucie?'

'Lucie's not his daughter.'

'Is that why you thought it was okay to treat her like dirt and trick her into believing she was in love with my brother?'

The dig landed. She saw it, the tightening of his features. 'Lucie agreed to marry your brother. I did not coerce her or bribe her or blackmail her. She agreed of her own volition, and then she let her emotions get the better of her and broke her word—we all knew how things would end if she failed to marry Thanasis; it's what's playing out now. Her amnesia gave us all the chance to play the card again and if your brother hadn't been so damned stupid as to tell her the truth, she wouldn't have run again and your family wouldn't be facing bankruptcy.'

'And I wouldn't be sitting here.'

Now he was the one to consider what had just been said. 'Would you ever have told me about the baby if circumstance hadn't forced you into it?'

'Only out of obligation, but not before the baby was born.'

'What the hell does *out of obligation* mean?'

'I would have told you because you have a right to know and our child has a right to know its father, but I wouldn't have asked for anything from you or wanted or expected anything.'

Incredulity rang from his eyes. 'You think I wouldn't have heard about the pregnancy once you started showing?'

She had a small drink of her water, holding the glass tightly to stop him seeing the tremor in her hand. 'I'd planned to hide myself away after Lucie and Thanasis's wedding. I'm not one for the society social scene so no one would have missed my presence.'

'What about your family?' he asked in disbelief. 'How the hell did you think they were going to react when you told them? Your brother would have hunted me down.'

'I wasn't going to name the father to anyone until after the birth. My hope was that my parents would fall in love with the baby before I told them. I hoped that loving it would make it harder for them to turn their back on it.'

He put his cutlery down and pushed his plate to one side to lean forwards. 'Did you, at any point in all your plotting, consider my feelings and what I would have wanted?'

'Alexis, I was just another notch on your bedpost. If you hadn't taken me back to your apartment that night some other woman would have gone with you, and if you remembered me it would only be because of who I am and the fact that we didn't exactly part on good terms. I thought you'd be relieved to be let off the fatherhood hook.'

'Let off the fatherhood hook?'

For the first time since she'd known him, Lydia saw real anger on his face.

'Oh, come on,' she defended herself, gripping her forearm. 'I can't be the first woman you've had a condom mishap with. For all I know, there could be a dozen mini Alexises stashed away around Europe.'

'No, Lydia, there are no mini Alexises, not in Europe or anywhere. What you and I shared that weekend was *not normal*, do you not understand that?'

'You called me a *not particularly memorable one-weekend stand* only yesterday!' she protested.

His lips twisted. 'They were just words. In my world, what counts is actions and intentions, and your intention until your hand was forced otherwise was to keep me out of my child's life. You didn't even want me to share in the pregnancy with you.'

'Only because that's what I thought you'd want!'

He stared at her for the longest time, long enough for

her trembling insides to turn into a guilt-ridden quivering wreck. 'Then you don't know me at all.'

'Alexis...'

He cut her off with the scraping-back of his chair. 'I'm going to bed. I haven't slept for two days and need to sleep. Finish your meal and join me when you're ready—I choose to believe that it's sleep deprivation causing my dinner to taste so bitter.'

He disappeared inside without another word.

Lydia crept into the bedroom. She'd seriously debated finding another room to sleep in but didn't want to make matters worse. She'd angered Alexis enough as it was.

Her heavy heart twisted to see the dim bedside light left on for her. Twisted harder to see the huge form burrowed beneath the sheets and the flash of black hair poking out of the top.

In the bathroom, a toothbrush still in its packaging had been left on the ledge above the sink for her, and she brushed her teeth automatically, her head too full of the man she was about to slide under the sheets beside to even pay attention to the action of rinsing her mouth out.

Was it possible that she'd hurt him?

It had never crossed her mind that Alexis was capable of feeling something as everyday human as hurt, but, hurt or anger or both, it didn't matter, she'd caused it. Hurt or anger or both, she still felt wretched.

The heavy robe hung back on the door, she tiptoed to the bed holding tightly to her thrashing heart and carefully slipped under the covers.

It wasn't until she turned the light off and the only noise to be heard through the darkness was the blood roaring in her ears did she realise Alexis, his back turned to her, was still awake.

'I'm sorry,' she whispered, guilt driving her words. 'I shouldn't have made assumptions. I was…' Terrified. The positive sign on the pregnancy test had unleashed a swathe of emotions but terror had been the strongest, a future as a single mother without the family who'd always loved and protected her all she could see. Her family who were already having to deal with the prospect of losing everything.

The thought of tracking Alexis down a second time to tell him the news and what she'd believed would be the strong likelihood of him contemptuously offering to pay her off had terrified her too. The bad feelings they'd parted with had still tasted bitter in her mouth but, as hard as she'd tried, she'd been completely unable to stop her mind being consumed by him. Been completely unable, too, to stop her heart skipping and her stomach lurching every time her phone made a noise. Knowing the life growing inside her meant she would be tied to Alexis for the rest of her life…that had been the most terrifying thing of all.

She swallowed to force her next words out. 'I can make all the excuses in the world but I should have told you as soon as I knew.'

His silence spoke louder than any verbal answer could have done.

CHAPTER SIX

THE PALACE GATES opened for her, and in that brief moment Lydia felt like a bona fide princess. She'd seen plenty of pictures of the palace, one of Europe's largest, over the years, but nothing could have prepared her for its magnificence in the flesh. In a country with a strong shared cultural heritage with its Greek neighbour Crete, its palace had a strong Middle Eastern flavour to it, as if it had long ago been built for a great Sultan, its multicoloured turrets and domed roofs gleaming under the midday sun.

Driving slowly through the magnificent grounds, she feared her heart might smash its way out of her chest.

Would Alexis even be there?

She'd been gently woken by a maid with her laundered clothes and a tray of coffee, fruit and pastries. The bed had been empty, not even residual warmth on Alexis's side. But she'd caught the faint trace of his cologne lingering in the air and knew he must have showered and dressed in stealth mode. A kindness to let her sleep a little longer? Did he know that she'd still been wide awake hours after he'd fallen into a deep sleep, her thoughts wretched, longing for him to roll over and press into her, longing to roll over and press herself into him? Or was he still too angry to want to speak to her?

Once she'd finished eating, she'd been given a short brown wig to disguise herself with and a credit card, and then taken to Agon's swankiest hotel by Alexis's driver with strict instructions to be ready for collection in two hours.

Inside, she'd been astounded to find numerous boutiques catering to all tastes.

Lydia could never explain to herself why she hadn't grabbed the first pair of jeans and vaguely reasonable top to wear, nor why she'd bought makeup and perfume, nor why she'd spent so long in the guest shower room that she'd had to run to make it to the car park on time. Nor did she understand why she wrenched the wig off as soon as the driver closed the door and then spent half the journey frantically brushing and fiddling with her hair.

And she would never be able to explain or understand why the fear that had rooted itself so tightly in the knots in her belly was the fear that Alexis had changed his mind, and that no matter how much she rubbed her belly and whispered to the tiny life inside it that its daddy would be there, that he was committing himself to them, she couldn't shake off the even more deeply rooted fear that he would never commit himself solely to *her*.

As far as fears went, it was ludicrous because she'd loftily told him she didn't demand or expect fidelity and he'd never even alluded to it. She shouldn't want it. She shouldn't. She wouldn't.

Somehow she had to find a way to stop herself imagining him with other women. Learn to block her own thoughts, and, if that proved impossible, learn to control the sickness those thoughts always induced.

Be more Rebecca Tsaliki, she chanted to herself. Be more Rebecca Tsaliki.

If the palace itself had a Middle Eastern flavour, the royal chapel, its yellow walls excepted, was pure Greek.

Not a soul witnessed her slip through its doors. Only the prince, a mountain of a man bigger even than Alexis, his beautiful wife, Amelie, and the priest were there to greet her. And Alexis, standing at the altar…

Relief whooshed through every cell of her body. And something else, something that filled her chest and weakened her legs.

He met her at the aisle's halfway point. His face was a mask she couldn't read. 'I thought you might have done a Lucie.'

She had to clear her choked throat. 'I thought you might have done a Lucie too.'

His chest rose before a half-smile played on his lips, and she suddenly found herself overwhelmed with a longing to see the full-blown smile that had so warmed her the first time it had been bestowed on her all that time ago. 'We made a deal, my angel. Now it is time to seal it.'

Alexis recited his vows still expelling relief that Lydia hadn't fled from the hotel and taken the first flight off the island. Even though his driver had messaged when he was en route to the palace, he'd been unable to shake the feeling that the car would arrive empty. But she was here and so ravishingly beautiful that when she'd stepped into the chapel he'd felt her presence like a punch to his heart.

Having expected her to turn up in ripped jeans, and still furious that she'd believed he wouldn't want to be a father, his ego punched all over again at her scathing dismissal of their weekend together, he'd been tempted to wear something similar, only changing into smart navy trousers and a white shirt at the last minute for the sole reason that they were marrying in a house of God and so he should at least make an effort to look respectable.

The last thing he'd expected was for Lydia to make an effort too. She was so naturally beautiful that she didn't need to make an effort but when she did, the effect was breathtaking.

Far from wearing ripped jeans, she stood facing him at the altar in a creamy white floaty dress, the laced long-sleeved top half plunging in a V giving a hint of her growing cleavage, the flowing skirt ruched, the whole thing tied together with a thick brown belt at the waist. She looked like she should be running through a meadow with her long blonde hair trailing behind her.

Their vows made, the time had come to seal their marriage like they'd sealed their commitment to their deal of a real marriage—with a kiss.

Their eyes locked together. He pressed a hand into

the small of her back A small hand slid onto his shoulder. His heart thumping a roar in his head, Alexis brought his mouth down to hers as she lifted her mouth to his. He glimpsed a sweep of her lashes before he closed his eyes and their lips fused together in a long, lingering kiss.

Breaking apart, he gazed again into the hazel eyes now brimming with an emotion he'd never seen in them before.

Euphoria slammed through him.

Lydia was *his*.

She was married. A married woman. Married to Alexis Tsaliki.

God help her.

Prince Talos had arranged a wedding meal for them in a stateroom in the palace, the four of them dining at a table that could comfortably seat fifty.

She was dining with royalty, a thought that was only a dim whisper in a head filled wholly with the man seated next to her, eating, chatting and laughing as if this were all just an ordinary meal. Her husband.

The wedding service itself had passed in a daze but she could still feel the mark of Alexis's mouth from their kiss. Still feel the longing that had ripped through her when he'd made his vows, a swelling of emotion that had filled her so completely she had no memory of reciting her own identical vows in turn.

'I promise you love, honour and respect; to be faithful to you, and not to forsake you until death do us part...'

Why hadn't it occurred to her that marrying in a chapel would mean reciting traditional vows? And why, when the time had come to recite them, had it felt the most natural thing in the world when it was all a lie? As if Alexis were going to be faithful to her! As if he could ever love her! As if she could ever love him!

But it had all felt so natural and, in the moment, right, and now she had an impending sense of doom in the pit of her stomach that she'd just made the greatest mistake of her life.

A hand slid onto her thigh. She trembled as a jolt of electricity shot through her, and tightened her hold on the stem of her glass to stop herself seeking out the hand to hold it.

He was marking his territory, she told herself. Reminding her that *she* was now his territory, reminding her of what was to come when they left the palace, and she didn't know if her growing sickness was nerves, terror or excitement. All she did know was that her heart had forgotten how to beat properly and when his fingers made gentle circles on her thighs, she didn't know if she wanted to grab his hand to shove it off her or move it higher…

As desperately as she wished for time to slow down, it accelerated, their seven courses flashing by at such speed that before she knew it, she was being embraced by the prince and princess with wishes for a long and happy marriage that registered like a distant ringing in her ears. When she climbed into the back of the car she realised she couldn't remember a single thing she'd eaten or a single snippet of conversation.

Nerves hadn't just kicked in, they were doing a full-blown cancan with a vigour that only increased when their car set off.

They were returning to Alexis's apartment to consummate the marriage. To have sex. For Lydia to fulfil her side of their deal as Alexis had just fulfilled his.

A large, warm hand covered the fist she hadn't even realised she'd made. 'How are you feeling, *wife*?'

Terrified.

She tried to conjure a smile. 'Good. You?'

A slow smile curved his cheeks and he leaned his face closer to hers. 'Very good.'

It was the blaze of sensuality in his eyes and the promise contained in it that had her sharply extract her hands from his on the pretext of removing her phone from her bag and checking her messages. She couldn't bear the longing that swelled in her to see it.

Hugely aware of Alexis's silent displeasure at her abrupt turning from him, even more aware that she was close to falling to pieces, Lydia bowed her head and tried to focus on reading the myriad messages she'd received from her mother with updates, along with the myriad messages from friends wanting to know what on earth was going on and why Thanasis and Lucie's wedding had been called off. And she tried harder than ever to block out the hunk of a man whose thigh was pressed against hers, and clear her body and mind of all the feelings and emotions ravaging her.

* * *

There was no preamble. They returned to the villa late afternoon and went straight up to the bedroom, Lydia's hand caught in Alexis's possessive hold.

He held the door open for her, then closed it firmly behind them, shutting out the world, narrowing it down to just the two of them.

Blue-grey eyes locked onto hers.

Lydia could no longer feel the individual beats of her heart. All efforts to clear her body and mind had come to nothing. The sickness in her stomach was like no sickness she'd ever felt before.

His stare fixed firmly on her, Alexis removed his watch and cufflinks and placed them on his dresser, then his fingers pinched the top button of his shirt. Working methodically, he undid the buttons one by one and shrugged his arms free.

She could swear her whole body contracted, and she drank him in, helpless to turn her stare away, helpless to stop her tongue tingling with the remembered taste of that glorious body, her breasts tightening in anticipation of being flattened against it.

There was a buzzing from inside the bag she was holding to her chest as if it were a life raft.

His eyes narrowed. 'Ignore it. You spent long enough on it in the car.'

Call it defiance, stubbornness, fear, anything, but she wrenched her stare from his and pulled her phone out. Before she could swipe to answer it, the phone had been plucked from her hand.

'Give it back, that's my mother calling.'

'No.' He placed it beside his watch on the dresser.

Fear turned to an anger she couldn't begin to understand. 'Give that back!'

'No. I have been more than patient but enough is enough.'

Anger morphing into fury, she charged past him, her stretched fingers about to clasp hold of the phone when an arm hooked around her waist and she was spun around and hauled flush into bare solid torso.

'What are you so afraid of?' he demanded harshly, his features as tight as she'd ever seen them, his stare boring down on her.

Everything.

'*Nothing,*' she spat, raising her arm; would have slapped him away if he hadn't caught her wrist.

'Good, then there is nothing to stop me doing this.' There was no time for her to even breathe let alone brace herself before his mouth came crushing down on hers.

In an instant, the foundations of Lydia's world moved as Alexis's dark taste filled her, his kiss a skilled, ruthless assault of the senses that knocked all the air from her lungs and all the sense from her brain.

His features were still taut when he broke the fusion, but his eyes…his eyes burned with an intensity she'd never seen in them before, trapping her even more tightly to the force of his will.

Nostrils flaring, he clasped her waist and lifted her

off her feet, wordlessly carrying her to the bed where he laid her down and pinned her beneath him.

His gorgeous but implacable face loomed down on her. 'I ask you again, what are you so frightened of?'

But she was too choked on the heat his savage kiss had unleashed in her and too overwhelmed with all the other feelings careering through her to answer.

His face contorted although with what she couldn't say, could only feel it, almost like a pain in her heart.

'No more hiding from me, Lydia. No more fighting me. We made our vows and now you are mine, do you understand that?'

The brutality of his words and ferocity in his stare should have made her quail but instead it melted something in her, something deep in her core that made her breathe out a sigh and mutely plead with him to understand that it wasn't him she was fighting but herself because...

Because he was going to break her heart.

The realisation hit her straight in the heart he was going to break.

Staring with equal intensity into the eyes boring into hers brought another truth. She was already in too deep. Even if she hadn't conceived his child she would have struggled to forget him, but she *had* conceived, a part of him combining with a part of her and taking life, and now she carried him everywhere she went. In her womb, in her blood, in her head, in her dreams.

It was all too late. Alexis was already a part of her and he was going to break her heart and there was nothing she could do about it because this was the deal she'd made.

He was giving her everything she'd asked for. He'd married her when he could have said no. He hadn't disputed their child's paternity, hadn't even questioned it. The only thing he'd played hardball over was their marriage being a real one, and she'd agreed to it. She'd agreed to *this* because, deep down inside, it was what she wanted too. She'd just been too frightened to admit it to herself, and now all she could do was her best to protect the parts of her he hadn't yet touched because she couldn't keep fighting against a future that was already written, a future she'd agreed to, sealed with a kiss that had burned her into fondue and which still lingered in her veins.

Her throat still too choked to speak, she raised her hand and cupped his cheek.

He closed his eyes and breathed in deeply. After long, long moments, he recaptured her stare. The hard intensity that had blazed in his eyes softened. 'Our families might be at war, but I am not your enemy. I never have been. I am your husband and you are my wife. It's you and me now, Lydia, and that's how it will always be.'

When his mouth came back down on hers it was with a driven sense of purpose. Fingers dragged through her hair as his tongue parted her lips in an intimate, demanding exploration that sparked electricity into all her senses and opened her up like the petals of a flower blossoming under the sun.

Alexis was her sun, she thought dimly as their kiss

deepened and all the passion she'd tried so hard and for so long to contain ignited into an inferno. The sun that breathed life into a body that had never known such pleasure existed.

It was only when Lydia's fingers burrowed into his hair and clasped his skull to fuse their mouths even tighter that the last of the tightness in Alexis's chest breathed free and he allowed himself to let go.

Burrowing his face into the delicate skin of her neck, he breathed Lydia deeply into his lungs, filling himself with the scent and taste he'd been unable to shake since she'd left his bed, and when she gave a soft moan, he drank it through his pores with the same greed.

She was his now, and he was going to make it so damned good for her that she'd never want to leave his bed or his life again.

Lifting himself off her, he straddled her thighs and, without any ceremony, unbuckled her belt. That discarded with, it was easy to slide the sleeves of her dress off her shoulders and then pull it down... *Theos*, she wasn't wearing a bra. Her succulent, perfect breasts with the rosy-red peaks were bare. A deep throb of lust speared him and, unable to resist a taste, he swooped down and captured a breast in his mouth in the way that had driven her so wild before.

Lydia arched her neck and cried out at the tight sensation, and she thrust her chest up and cradled his head, but he was intent on torturing her, moving his mouth down and trailing his tongue over her stomach as he tugged her dress over her hips. With a lift of her bottom, he pulled it down, past her thighs and then roughly dragged it to her feet and threw it to one side before sliding her knickers down and discarding them too.

Making quick work of his remaining clothes, he stretched out on top of her, the tips of her breasts jutting against the hardness of his chest as he cupped her face. 'You will never know what you do to me,' he whispered, and then his hands and mouth were everywhere, touching, kissing, biting, inflaming her skin, inflaming her veins, seeking, searching...and the hot restlessness deep in her core took possession of her until she was nothing but a boneless mass, a creature of pleasure, created for this man and this man alone.

Hands capturing her wrists, his mouth found her breasts again, and all she could do was writhe helplessly as his tongue encircled her peaks, licking and tasting, teasing, teasing, teasing...

'Please,' she gasped. *'Please.'*

Just when she thought she couldn't take the torture any longer, he took a peak into his mouth and released her wrists to slide his hands down the curves of her inflamed body as he suckled, giving her the pleasure she so craved, a pleasure she'd never even known she could feel until she'd fallen hedonistically into Alexis's bed and he'd shown her just how exquisite pleasure could be.

Moving his attention to her other sensitised breast, his fingers trailed over her stomach and then slipped between her legs.

There was a moment of delicious anticipation where she stopped breathing entirely, a faint groan from his throat as he cupped her heat and then he slid a finger inside her and she couldn't hear anything above the roar in her ears.

It was as though she were caught in a fever with his mouth moving relentlessly over her breasts and his fingers sliding in and out of her until, as if he really had been teasing her, he found the centre of where she throbbed unmercifully and, with barely any pressure from his thumb, she erupted, crying out, her hands flailing as her climax took her to the dimension only Alexis could carry her to.

The waves of her climax hadn't even begun to subside when he snaked his way back up her throat to kiss her, reigniting her passion with little more than his taste.

Mouths fused together all over again, she raised her hips and writhed, desperately seeking his full possession, barely felt him capturing her wrists again and pressing them at the side of her head until he broke the fusion of their lips.

Opening her eyes, she found his hooded gaze boring down on her, his breathing heavy.

'Tell me you're mine,' he demanded roughly.

Her throat caught.

He brought his face right to hers so the tips of their noses touched. His arousal was pressing where she most needed it to be but no matter how much she strained her pelvis in a silent plea for him to just *take her*, his stare continued to uncompromisingly drill into her. 'Say it. Say it, Lydia. Tell me you're mine.'

In such a fevered state she'd have said anything,

promised anything if he would only just *take her*, she parted her lips. 'I...' And then her words cut away as she found herself trapped in his stare, not just trapped in it but carried into it, like an invisible piece of herself had dislodged and transferred into his possession.

She lifted her head and pressed her mouth to his. Eyes still locked together, she whispered, 'I'm yours, Alexis.'

There was a long moment of stillness before he expelled a long groan into her mouth, and then buried himself deep, deep inside her.

Lydia had carried the sensation of his lovemaking all these long months but time must have diminished it because *this*...

His hot, demanding tongue danced into her mouth and she was lost.

Closing her eyes, she returned his kisses with the same passionate intensity, holding him tightly as she spread her legs even wider and submitted herself to the magic of his lovemaking.

Alexis could hardly hold on. All these months he'd carried their lovemaking in his head but memory had nothing on reality and now he was an electrified coil straining against release, but, *Theos*, the sensation...

She was close to the edge. He could feel it, the delicious tension coiling through her body, the heightened colour on her cheeks when she flung her head back, the tightness of her fingers when they gripped hold of his biceps, the straining sinews of her delicate neck, the growing thickness around his arousal as he drove in and out of her…and then her eyes flew open.

With her lips parted and her hazel stare locked onto his in wonder, the contractions of her release pulled him deeper and deeper until he was thrusting into her with all his frenzied power and his own coil snapped and he came with a load roar of her name.

CHAPTER SEVEN

EVEN THOUGH HE'D propped himself onto an elbow to stop Lydia having to take the full brunt of his weight, a sneaking fear that he could still hurt her and the baby propelled Alexis to move off her. He was still trying to catch his breath. Could still feel the tremors of her body. Hell, he could still feel the tremors of *his* body.

Rolling onto his back, he hooked an arm beneath her and drew her to him.

There was the slightest resistance before she rested her head on his chest and curled into him. Sweat glistened off both their bodies.

He held her tightly and closed his eyes. His thoughts were fragmented, his emotions shot.

'I can hear your heartbeats,' she whispered into the silence.

Cupping her neck, he burrowed his fingers into her hair. 'I can feel yours.' An erratic thud right beneath where her soft breasts were pressing into him, and his loins twitched in response. *Theos*, he could hardly believe fresh arousal was already snaking its way through him... No, he could believe it. Believe it because he'd already lived it, that one hedonistic weekend where unashamed raw desire had ballooned into a passion that had blown his mind.

A need to just *look* at her had him gently manipulating her onto her back and stretching himself over her.

Being careful not to press too much of his weight on her, he soaked in the beautiful face and then pressed a light kiss to the lips swollen from the passion of their lovemaking. 'Are you okay?'

Hazel eyes holding his, she gave the tiniest smile and nodded, and rested her hand at the nape of his neck.

He kissed her again. 'Are you hungry?'

She shook her head and sighed before lifting her head to kiss him. 'Not for food.'

It wasn't possible that he could be hard again so soon but he was, and when she kissed him again, sliding inside her felt the most natural thing in the world.

Lydia opened her eyes to find herself entwined in Alexis's arms and the room bathed in a dusky light that told her the sun would soon be lost to the horizon.

Gently trying to extract herself from his hold without waking him, she was foiled from escaping when he tightened the arm around her waist.

'Where do you think you're going?' he murmured sleepily.

'The bathroom.'

He sighed as if being put upon. 'Okay, I suppose I can allow that.'

'You are too kind.'

'I know.'

Giggling softly, she lifted her head to kiss him, her chaste display of affection morphing into a full-blown passionate kiss when Alexis's fingers speared her hair and his tongue slid into her mouth.

After what felt like a bucketful of kisses, she finally wriggled free and managed to make her liquid legs carry her to the bathroom.

There was a semi-stranger looking back at her in the bathroom mirror. Lydia had met her only once before: the morning after her second night with Alexis. Then, she had gazed at her reflection with sorrow clutching her heart that the most magical time of her life had to end, a little bit like she'd felt as a child when all the lights from the Christmas and New Year celebrations were taken down and all the joy they represented was packed away for what had felt to young Lydia as interminably long months. Quickly, though, that flattening of her spirits would dissipate and life would return to normal.

Life had never returned to normal after her weekend with Alexis. Her spirits had never lifted themselves back to normal levels. She'd carried a flatness in her soul she'd never been able to shake.

Now she looked at the semi-stranger, a woman with glowing eyes and rosy cheeks, and wondered why she'd never met her before Alexis. And couldn't help but wonder when she would disappear and the Lydia who'd always looked back at her would reappear, the Lydia who loved her family dearly but who'd always yearned for something different for herself but had never quite found the courage to go out and get it without detaching the safety nets they provided.

There was nothing safe about Alexis. He came without a safety net. He might dress in suits like her father and brother but he was thrilling and dangerous, everything they weren't, and he was going to break her heart.

She'd made her choice and she wouldn't lie to herself that she'd made it because she had no choice. She'd agreed to this, and she could spend their marriage hating him and fighting him and making them both miserable, or she could take what they did have together and just enjoy it for as long as it lasted. So long as she kept herself clear-sighted about what *this* was then she'd be able to protect the parts of her heart Alexis hadn't yet touched, and then when the time came for her to lie in the bed of her own making she'd be able to lie in it stoically and without complaint. Or at least try.

Back in the bedroom, she crossed to the bed wondering why she didn't feel any shyness about her naked body in front of him. She knew she had an okay figure but she'd never had that body confidence so many other women had and had never been comfortable with parading her nakedness in front of her partners. But then, they'd never looked at her with such naked appreciation and lust as Alexis did, as he was looking at her now. As if she were the biggest present left under the Christmas tree.

She was about to climb back into bed when her phone started buzzing.

She sighed. She'd had a dim awareness of her phone going off numerous times over the last few hours, reality doing its best to intrude.

'Ignore it,' he urged, throwing the sheets back and reaching an arm out to her. 'This is our wedding night.'

Torn, she bit into her bottom lip. 'It might be important.'

Eyes gleaming, he pointed to the huge erection he was sporting. 'More important than this?'

She couldn't help but laugh, even as the spot between her legs throbbed.

The amusement on his face dimmed a little and he expelled a long breath.

'What's wrong?' she asked.

He shook his head. 'Just thinking that's the first time you've laughed since I saw you again.' That flicker in his eyes made a brief return. 'I was starting to fear I'd never hear it again.'

'A man like you?' she said lightly to mask the tendrils of her heart tightening. 'I didn't think you were scared of anything.'

His stare was serious. 'Neither did I.' And then a smile curved his lips and with a speed and agility no man of his size should have, he twisted over and caught her by the waist, lifting her onto the bed and pulling her on top of him. 'Now I've got you.'

Laughing, she tried to wriggle off, might have succeeded if he hadn't captured a breast in his mouth.

'Alexis…' Her protest died in her throat as a surge

of electrical desire pulsed straight from her breast into her groin.

His mouth now snaking up her neck, he found her lips and kissed her passionately.

'Let's have this one night,' he murmured huskily, his fingers skimming down her back to grope the cheek of her bum. 'Forget the world and our families and just live for now.'

By the time he drove inside her, she'd forgotten anyone else existed but Alexis.

Lydia stood on the balcony of Alexis's room gazing out at the peaceful lapping of the sea on his private beach. They could be the only two people in existence.

She sighed. 'Do we really have to go back?'

Arms slid around her waist, a hard body pressing into her back. 'One day of marriage and already you are selfish for me,' he murmured, almost purring like a satisfied cat.

She was glad he couldn't see her expression at his jovial arrogance or he would recognise the truth in his words. 'As amazing a lover as you are, I was thinking more about everything we've got coming for us when we get back to Athens.'

His mouth brushed her ear, a hand cupping her breast. 'You think I'm an amazing lover?'

A delicious shiver ran up her spine. 'With all your experience there would be something wrong if you weren't.'

He playfully pinched her nipple. 'You do love cutting me down to size,' he mused, sliding his hand back down to her stomach and resting his chin on her head. 'I'm not afraid to say that I'm entirely selfish for you and if I could extend our time here then I would, but there are too many fires to put out.'

Lydia's heart should *not* sigh at his admittance of being selfish for her. Alexis was sex mad. The difference between them was that she was only sex mad for him and she would rather dye her hair blue than admit this or admit he was the first man to have ever made her climax. Alexis's ego did not need feeding.

Determined not to let her mood slip, she lightly said, 'Don't you employ staff to put fires out for you?'

'I do, and they've been fighting them since we got here, but it's not fair for me to expect them to do it any longer. I took control of Tsaliki Shipping from my father with the promise that I would turn its future around for the better. Now that things have gone to hell, I can't leave it to others. It's my responsibility to fix things, no one else's.'

Not wanting to think of her brother battling the same fires but with no hope of extinguishing them, Lydia leaned back into Alexis and closed her eyes. It was time to face her immediate future head-on. 'Where will I go?'

'What do you mean?'

'When we're back in Athens. I suppose I should go home—'

'Your home is with me,' he cut in firmly.

'But we're not going to be announcing our news until

Sunday. What am I supposed to do until then? Just hide away?' She couldn't be seen around Athens. Her face wasn't well known like Alexis's or her brother's, but all the recent publicity had put her in a spotlight she'd never been under before, and there was always the chance she'd bump into someone or be seen by someone who actually knew her and knew her family. While her parents had been glad of her supposed trip to England and its means of getting her safely out of the media's firing line, how could she justify being back in her home city and not going home to them? Just to imagine the turmoil they were all going through made her feel wretched. Knowing she'd married Alexis to save her own skin made her feel worse, a feeling that didn't change when she reminded herself she'd done it for their baby's sake or when she reminded herself that as soon as she was in a position to help, she'd be there for them.

She still hadn't checked her phone. Barely a whole day had passed since Alexis had swiped it from her hands and now the thought of scrolling through her messages filled her with dread. Her mother would be going out of her mind.

'It's only for six days,' he said. 'Anything you need to entertain you by day will be provided.' He dipped his mouth back to her ear. 'And I'll be home to provide a very different kind of entertainment by night.'

Just to imagine it was enough to fill her with longing and for her legs to weaken. The jut of his arousal poking through his shorts and into the small of her back wasn't helping, and when she clamped her hands to his to stop them wandering back to her breasts, she held them tightly in part to stop herself from dragging his hands back up to them.

'I still need my clothes,' she reminded him. As sensually erotic as it felt to wear Alexis's shirts, she wanted her own stuff.

'I'll have them collected and brought to the apartment. Give me your friend's address and I'll make the arrangements now.'

'Is this always your approach to solving problems? Just get on and sort it?' Not just problems but things he wanted. He'd wanted her and he'd had her. He'd wanted a real marriage and within two days he'd got his wish. When Alexis wanted something to happen, he made it happen.

'What other way is there to approach them?'

'I don't know. Until the war between our fathers hit the news and everything imploded, I lived a charmed life. Everything was easy. I never wanted for anything.' And, she was starting to suspect, it was fear of actually wanting for something that had stopped her cutting the safety net her family provided. Maybe all this was a punishment for being so complacent about her place in life. 'What gave you your drive? Why were you the only Tsaliki offspring to get out there and make a name and fortune for himself off his own back?'

He exhaled heavily into her hair and when he spoke, it was without the sensual undertone that had been lacing his voice the whole conversation. 'Because I didn't want to be my father.'

That was not an answer she'd been expecting.

'I grew up wanting to be him,' he explained quietly. 'I idolised him. When he divorced my mother and I was told I'd be staying primarily with my father, I was glad.'

'How old were you?'

'Eight, and it took me another twelve years to realise my father is actually a narcissistic arsehole who uses his money as a weapon. He paid my mother and my first two stepmothers off and God knows how many mistresses. I'm one of nine and I'm quite sure there would be more of us if Rebecca hadn't forced him to have a vasectomy after Loukas was born. He likes to keep everyone close, one big happy family all feeding his ego and living off his largesse, but all it does is create a cycle of dependence and allows him to get away with and justify any kind of behaviour.'

'So how were you able to see through him if your siblings haven't?'

'I'm quite sure all my siblings have seen through him too but they're happy to be props in Georgios Tsaliki's tapestry of what a great, generous man he is. I wasn't.'

'But *why*? What made you different?'

'Partly it's to do with being the oldest. I'm thirty-seven and can remember a time when it was just my father, my mother, Constantine, Atticus and me. This was before Dad really made a success of the business and traded my mother in and our lives became a circus.'

'Did you see much of your mother after the divorce?'

'I saw her all the time. My father's a generous man

and bought her a house close to ours. She would often join us on holidays too. Our relationship's a good one.'

'I'm glad.'

'See?' he said in a lighter tone. 'I *can* sustain a relationship with a woman.'

Lydia cut through the wave of sadness Alexis's snippet about his early childhood had provoked by forcing a small laugh at a jest that made the sadness heavier. 'You said you're different from your siblings in your drive partly because you're the oldest. Does that mean there was something else at play?'

'Yes, and that something was your father.'

His words hung between them until he said, 'Lydia, I grew up believing the Antoniadis name was synonymous with the devil. You were all vultures who'd built your fortune off the back of my father's work. As my father would tell it, he was the brains in the partnership between himself and your father, and when your father severed it, he took all the best contacts and systems my father had put in place leaving my father to start again from nothing. I still don't know the truth of this and I doubt I ever will because both men tell a different story, but when I was twenty I passed your father in the street and I was curious, mostly because he didn't have devil horns in his head.'

'My father's a good man,' she said quietly.

'He behaved as badly as my father during their war but I believe that fundamentally he's a better man than him. Seeing him sparked something in me and I started asking about him with contacts, just to get an outside perspective, and all I heard were good things. A good man, a good and fair employer. No scandals, no illegitimate children, no largesse... I'm not saying learning about your father made me want to be like him because I was twenty and his life sounded as exciting as magnolia paint, but it was one of those lightbulb moments—that my father wasn't the great man I'd always believed, that he was actually selfish and venal and that I was on the path to becoming a carbon copy of him. It just sparked in me a whole new perspective of my father and myself, and it also made me realise I was completely dependent on him and that if I didn't do something about it, I would be dependent on him for the whole of my life. It lit the fire in me to find my own path and make my own mark on the world.'

Lydia held the hand pressed against her belly, digesting all Alexis had just revealed to her and thinking, too, about how her desire to find her own path outside the family business had extended only as far choosing graphic design over shipping and moving into the cottage at the bottom of the family garden. The Antoniadis Shipping shares assigned to her had been deliberately designed to give her a modest income that would need to be supported by her own endeavours, but, in reality, she'd never really *had* to work. She'd had the same kind of expensive education as Alexis but she'd done little with it. Everything about her was modest, from her income to her home—which wasn't even hers—to her car, to the few boyfriends she'd chosen, nothing to set her alight or put a fire in her belly, her existence entirely forgettable.

How had she never seen that before?

No one could ever forget Alexis. He had a fire in *his* belly, an inner spark that shone brightly and drew people to him like moths to bask in the heat of his flame. Lydia had been drawn to that fire from the first lock of their eyes, and now she couldn't help herself fearing just how badly she would be burned from it.

Not wanting to think about the future she'd chosen to walk into, she said, 'How did you do it?'

'My father refused to give me or my siblings shares in the company because he didn't want to cede any potential control to us, but he paid me a good salary. I started investing it.' He laughed but there was little humour behind it. 'One thing I didn't expect was that he would respect me for it and that in itself spurred me on further. When you get to know my father you'll learn he has a real magnetism. Basking under his approval makes you feel like the king of the world. He's a man full of contradictions and my feelings for him are just as contradictory. For all his selfishness and narcissism, he has a generous heart.'

But in that moment she couldn't have cared less about contradictions or generous hearts. 'You want me to get to know him?' she asked in horror.

'You will get to know all my family,' he said calmly, as if this were nothing at all.

'But...they will hate me.'

His voice hardened. 'Some of them might—Athena

is a given, but she hates everyone—but if they want to stay on my good side, they will treat you with courtesy and respect or face the consequences.'

'I can't come between you and your family!'

'*You* are my family now, angel. You are my wife and you are carrying my child. That makes you more important to me than anyone.'

The most important person until the novelty wore off, she thought wretchedly but didn't say.

If there was one trait of his father Alexis had enthusiastically embraced, it was his womanising, and to endure it she was going to have to play the role of Alexis's stepmother, Rebecca Tsaliki. It wouldn't happen just yet, not while the chemistry was so strong, but it would happen, and she really must stop thinking about it otherwise the future with Alexis that had been prewritten would start to eat at her before it had even been lived.

'My family will never accept you or our child and I have nothing to threaten them with to force them,' she said miserably. 'In a week's time I'm going to be lucky if they let me keep the Antoniadis name.'

His hands moved from her stomach and slid up her arms to her shoulders and gently turned her around. Tilting her chin with his fingers, he quietly said, 'Lydia, I'm not going to pretend I don't know what's at stake for you or that things are going to be easy for you, but, whatever happens, you are not alone. Know that. We're in this together.' And then, as if to prove his point, his mouth came down on hers and he proved just how together they were.

CHAPTER EIGHT

THERE WAS REAL apprehension weighing down Lydia's chest when they took the elevator from Alexis's apartment block's underground car park up to his penthouse, and it had nothing to do with being hidden away in it for the best part of a week to look forward to. Her apprehension came from meeting his staff. Three months ago his butler had been on duty when they'd arrived back from the club and had been the one to deliver food to their room, while a maid had directed her to the elevator that took her down to the block's lobby when she'd done the *walk of shame* as Alexis had called it. She didn't know what would be worst—seeing or not seeing a flicker of recognition. If they didn't recognise her then she really had been just another interchangeable face to emerge from Alexis's bedroom, but if they did then she would have to live with them thinking God knew what about her. She knew she shouldn't care what strangers thought of her but she did care, deeply.

'You're sure your staff can be trusted to keep their mouths shut about me?' she whispered, as if the elevator had hidden microphones the staff were listening in on.

If he was annoyed at having to answer the same question for the thousandth time, he hid it well. 'I pay them too well to talk and even if they wanted to, the non-disclosure agreements they've all signed are watertight,' he reassured her for the thousandth time.

'I'm sorry. I just couldn't bear for my family to hear about us from anyone but me.'

He squeezed her hand. 'They won't.'

The elevator door opened and they stepped into the small, unfurnished room she had only the vaguest memory of.

'Tomorrow, I will have your eye-print added and give you all the access codes to the building,' he said, indicating the retinal scanner beside the reinforced steel door. 'It will allow you to come and go as you please.'

'I won't be going anywhere for a week, but thanks.'

'If you find yourself getting cabin fever you can always go out in that brown wig.'

'I'd rather not risk it, but thanks.'

'The option's there if you want it.'

'Thanks.'

Instead of putting his eye to the scanner, he narrowed his gaze. 'What's wrong?'

'Nothing?'

He raised both black eyebrows. 'I can feel your tension. What's wrong? Tell me or else I can't fix it.'

She smiled, the weight lifting a fraction. 'Alexis, you can't fix everything.'

'Want to bet?'

'Some things I have to fix myself. I'm worried about

what your staff are going to think about me, which is a me problem not a you or them problem.'

His stare held hers, that flicker in his eyes making a blink-and-you'll-miss-it appearance, and then he smiled and pressed a chaste kiss to her mouth. 'My staff will love you, I promise.'

He put his eye to the scanner. The green light flashed and the door opened, taking them through to the first of the many sprawling reception rooms in his impressive apartment. Not that Lydia had paid much attention to the apartment during her one visit to it before—on the way in they'd been too intent on making it to the bedroom for her to notice anything and on the way out she'd been too intent on just leaving without bursting into tears to take in any of the décor or furnishings.

The weight in her chest lifted a fraction more to find warmth in the eyes of the staff she was introduced to. The maid who'd shown her the way out wasn't there but the butler was, and, though she caught recognition from him, the warmth of his welcome was enough to put her fears in this regard to bed.

'Your cases have been delivered and unpacked for you,' the butler said once the others had disappeared.

'Already?' There wasn't much difference in flight times from Kos to Athens as from Agon to Athens, but she'd only given Maya's details to Alexis a couple of hours ago.

'You should know by now that I only employ the best people,' Alexis murmured. 'Let me show you the rest of the place and then we can shower before dinner.'

It came as no surprise that the two-storey apartment was a strong contender for the Ultimate Bachelor Pad of the Year award, coming complete with games room, cinema room and party room—the disco ball on the ceiling away gave its purpose—that were all interlinked with bars in each of them. The main living areas were all high ceilings, sash windows, dark leather sofas and glass tables. Everywhere they went were splashes of original pop art, from Warhols and Hockneys to colourful, eye-popping work created by more modern, contemporary artists.

'You can study them all tomorrow,' Alexis said, tugging at her hand when Lydia found herself enthralled with an utterly bonkers red apple on a seesaw. 'I've got a surprise for you.'

'What surprise?'

He gave her a stare. 'It wouldn't be a surprise if I told you, would it?'

They took the marble stairs to the top floor where Alexis's bedroom was, but instead of going through its door, they carried on past other doors to the end of the wide, light corridor. He flung the final door open for her with a flourish.

To Lydia's bemusement, she'd been shown to an office. A very nice office, with three huge desktop computers set out on a horseshoe desk, a coffee machine, sofa and six more pieces of pop art on the walls, and with an amazing view of the Acropolis. She assumed it was the view that was the surprise because she could think of nothing less thrilling than an office.

'What do you think?' he asked, staring at her with a tiny bit more intensity than the occasion called for.

She returned his intensity. 'It's the best office in the whole wide world.'

His brow furrowed and then he burst out laughing. 'I'm not showing you this for the sake of it—I'm showing you it because it's yours.'

Now it was Lydia's turn to furrow her brow. 'What do you mean by mine?'

'*Your* office, to work on your designs or play solitaire or whatever you want to do in it. I've had it on good authority that these computers are the best for your line of work but if they don't suit your needs or are not to your taste or liking we can change them...'

'Wait,' she interrupted. 'Are you telling me you've created an office for me?'

'And I thought you were quick on the uptake.'

'Alexis, I only agreed to marry you on Friday.' Although she supposed it would technically have been Saturday. 'Today is Monday.'

'Yes, it gave my staff plenty of time to arrange it all. Once we've broken the news of our marriage to the world we can get an interior designer in to discuss what else you'd like to do with it and colour schemes of how you'd like the rest of the place to look and feel.'

'The rest of the place?' she said faintly.

'This is now your home and it needs to feel like yours too or you will never be comfortable here.'

But there was no time to digest any of this for, without any warning whatsoever, Alexis had scooped her into his arms and was marching her down the corridor.

'What are you doing?'

He grinned. 'What I would have done yesterday if I hadn't thought you'd punch me—carrying you over the threshold.'

It was the brightness of the room that stopped Lydia from planting the intended kiss on his mouth.

In utter disbelief, she turned her head from left to right as far as her neck would extend.

The last time she'd been in this room it had been an unashamed bachelor's bedroom with seduction unashamedly in mind, with luxurious charcoal panelling and black silk sheets on a waterbed so big that if it had burst they'd have had to swim to safety. Other than the layout, nothing remained. Now, the walls were painted a soft eggshell green and cream, the bed of equal size but with a wrought-iron frame and luxurious cream and gold bedding that matched the new drapes hanging on the windows and the new, lighter, hardwood flooring...

This was a different room, she realised with a sinking heart. She'd been so desperate to leave the last time she'd been here that she'd remembered the position of the room wrongly.

'I thought I was going to be sharing your room,' she said, trying not to let her dejection show as he carried her to the bed. Dejection over something that just a day ago had been what she'd wanted. If she hadn't become so lust-struck she'd be celebrating this turn of events.

He laid her down and stretched on top of her. 'You are. This is it. Do you like it?'

'What, this is your room?'

'*Our* room now,' he corrected. 'But formerly my room.'

She wriggled out from under him so she could take it all in again and wrap her head around what she was seeing...

He propped himself on an elbow. 'Anything you don't like, we can change.'

'No, no, it's lovely, it's just...so different.'

Unsure from her expression and tone what she really meant, Alexis stared more closely at her and dubiously asked, 'Did you prefer it as it was?'

She gave a bark of surprised laughter. 'God, no! It was awful!' Colour stained her cheeks and she quickly added, 'I mean, it wasn't particularly to my taste.'

He smiled wryly. 'I didn't imagine it was and that's why I had it all changed.'

'What? All this has changed since Saturday?'

He stroked her soft cheek and said words that told a version of the truth. 'When I knew I would be marrying, I set things in motion.' Putting his mouth to her ear, he seductively whispered, 'How about we christen the bed before we shower?'

She pulled her head back to stare at him wonderingly. 'Do you mean...?'

He smiled at the movement of her throat when she couldn't finish her question. 'No one else has slept in this bed.' He laced his voice with meaning. 'This is our room and our bed and no one else will ever sleep in it but us.' He gave a wider smile and slid his hand down to her belly. 'I suppose we can let our baby share with us on occasion.'

To his incredulity, water filled her eyes and a tear spilled down her cheek. Palming the cheek, he wiped the tear with his thumb. 'I thought this would make you happy.'

Blinking back more tears, she bit into her bottom lip and gave a shaky smile. 'It does. I'm just feeling a bit emotional—probably tiredness and baby hormones.'

He gazed at her intently. 'You are sure that's all it is?'

She nodded and wrapped her arms around him, nestling her cheek into his shoulder. 'I'm sure. What you've done in here is beautiful.'

He held her tightly, breathing in the scent of her hair and rubbing his hands over her back, and assuring himself that she was here, that Lydia *was* his and that given time she would understand the fullness of what that meant...

And understand that he was hers too.

The weight Lydia had entered Alexis's apartment with had become heavier overnight and now, hugging her knees on the bed and watching him dress for the office, she could swear she felt it all the way down to her toes.

It was time for reality to pierce the bubble they'd made for themselves. It already had. It hadn't occurred to her that in all the time they'd spent together he must have turned his phone off because it was currently leaping around on his dresser like a jumping jack.

'Are you not going to answer it?' she asked, trying not to sound wistful.

He met her stare in the reflection of the mirror he was doing his tie up in front of and shook his head. 'I've seen and heard enough. The rest can wait until I'm in the car.'

'I suppose I should look at my phone too,' she sighed and flopped her head back on the pillow. 'Anything I should be prepared for?'

'Lucie's still in hiding. The press are still stalking your brother.' He grimaced and dipped his fingers into a pot on his dresser and rubbed his hands together before dragging it through his black hair. 'A rumour was published overnight on one of those British gossip sites that Lucie ran away to escape a forced marriage.'

Lydia's heart sank. 'Which site?'

He told her. It was a name that meant nothing to her.

'I've instructed my lawyers to get it taken down but…' He closed his eyes a moment. 'Once a rumour is out there it can be impossible to stop it taking on a life of its own. I've had my fair share of lies and innuendoes published. Normally I ignore them but this one…' He shook his head. 'This one has the potential to cause real damage.'

She thought of the woman she'd seen on the supply boat early Friday morning, when she'd still been working out how she was going to manage three days on Sephone avoiding all contact with Alexis. She'd dreaded it, had felt sick to the pit of her stomach to imagine even glimpsing him. It had been bad enough seeing his face all over the media on a near daily basis. Worse that in a few moments of weakness she'd searched his name herself. Worse still that the algorithms on the social media sites she used had kicked in, and, along with all the graphic-design-related posts, art, music and book posts curated to her specific tastes, had started infecting her feed with posts about Alexis Tsaliki. It meant that since their night together she'd been subjected to regular pictures of him dining and partying with a variety of beautiful women. If anything, his libido had become even more ravenous. There had been three different women in the last month alone.

And that was why she'd kept her mouth shut about Lucie being on the supply boat. If Lucie had needed to run then let her run free, even if one of the consequences of Lucie's freedom had been Lydia's own entrapment with the man she'd hoped to hide away from for ever. Or at least until their baby was born and all the feelings their night together had brought out in her had had the good sense to disappear.

'You'll be safe though, won't you?' she asked, now trying not to sound anxious.

'On a personal level, yes, but when it comes to Tsaliki Shipping...' He lifted his shoulders and grimaced again. 'You can only fight so many fires at one time. Too many and it becomes impossible to contain.' Striding to the bed, he leaned over and kissed her. 'I'll try not to be late but with everything going on, I can't guarantee it. Call me if you need me, okay?'

'Just go and fight your fires and don't worry about me.'

He smiled wryly. 'When I imagined marrying, I didn't imagine we'd only have a day for the honeymoon period.' Another kiss and then he was off, snatching his suit jacket from the armchair he'd draped it over, leaving Lydia puzzling over words that made no sense. They'd agreed to marry only four days ago and that was to put out Lydia's own fire, so why would he have imagined…?

A needle of ice injected itself into her heart.

Her brain working hard, she climbed off the bed and treaded her toes into the newly laid hardwood floor and thought back to the time she'd had contractors in to lay new flooring in her cottage. It had been a lot more involved than she'd initially envisaged. This bedroom was huge and the intricacy of the flooring design meant a specialist had been employed to lay it, and she just couldn't work out how Alexis's staff had found a specialist floor layer and employed them to remove the old stuff and then prep and lay the new stuff to this specific design in a maximum of three days.

Despite the warm welcome she'd received on her arrival, Lydia was still apprehensive about leaving the bedroom. Hunger drove her out. Feeling very much like a house guest abandoned by the owner, she headed to the kitchen she'd been given only a cursory tour of and found the chef already busy preparing for the evening dinner.

Once she'd got over her shock at being addressed as *despina*, a term she was used to associating with her mother, who was the lady boss of her household—Lydia absolutely did not feel like a *despina*—she still felt too much like a guest to say she'd find herself something to eat as she always did at home. Her parents employed chefs too but once she'd moved into the cottage, she'd had the urge to learn to cook for herself. While she would never win any culinary prizes, *strapatsada* for breakfast was the one meal she'd mastered to suit her own taste buds, especially since she'd become pregnant.

Hurried footsteps were followed by the flustered appearance in the kitchen of the maid who'd shown Lydia out of the apartment three months earlier.

'My apologies, *despina*,' she said. 'I didn't hear you leave your room. Let me show you to the dining room—the table has been set for you...unless you prefer to eat somewhere else?' she added with a touch of anxiety.

'The dining room works fine for me, thank you.' Her words had barely left her mouth before she was being chivvied to the smaller of the two dining rooms.

Thinking wistfully of her sunny kitchen and the table she'd managed to wedge by the bay window where she ate every morning looking out over her own private patch of the Antoniadises' landscaped gardens, Lydia took her seat and stared at the abundance of food that had been set out for her. It was the kind of spread she'd woken to every morning of her childhood and adolescence when the family had come together for the one meal where it was just the four of them. It was a rare evening meal when it was just them, her parents' open table policy being taken advantage of by extended family, friends, business associates and even employees, the evening meal often feeling like an extended board meeting. Once she'd officially moved out to what was essentially the cottage at the bottom of the garden, Lydia had still joined them most evenings for dinner, and her heart clenched tightly as it suddenly occurred to her that she'd already enjoyed her last evening meal with them.

'Coffee, *despina*?'

She nodded, blinking back the sudden swell of tears and prodding at her eye to make it seem as though she had something caught in it. 'Yes, please. Sorry, what's your name?'

'Maya.'

Another Maya. Lydia's lungs opened a little wider. She'd never known a horrible Maya.

'Can I be of any further assistance?'

'I'm good, but thank you...actually there is one thing.' Before she could talk herself out of asking it, she said, 'The flooring in the bedroom is different from when I was last here.' No point pretending that she hadn't made the walk of shame with this woman. Mercifully, she wasn't feeling any judgy vibes from her. 'How long ago was the new floor laid?'

Maya's forehead furrowed a little. 'I think two, maybe three months ago. I can check.'

'Don't worry about doing that.' She dredged all the

brightness into her tone that she could muster. 'I was just curious—it's all so different from how I remember it.'

If the maid's face hadn't turned the colour of the tomatoes the chef would be using to make Lydia's *strapatsada*, there was a slim chance she would have pushed the timing of the new flooring and the other niggling things to the back of her mind, but Maya's bright red cheeks, tight lips and the way she was rubbing at her skirt told a story Lydia valiantly assured herself it was better to know now. The words Alexis had said before he'd distracted her by telling her the bed was brand new and so silently confirming he'd not shared it with any of his other lovers came back to her.

'When I knew I would be marrying, I set things in motion...'

The drastic change in his bedroom hadn't been for her sake. The wheels for the change had started turning weeks, even months before she'd begged him to marry her.

Whoever Alexis had imagined himself marrying, it hadn't been her.

CHAPTER NINE

ALEXIS RODE THE elevator up to his apartment with a mixture of emotions playing in his guts. His legal team's efforts to get the gossip about Lucie removed had been as pointless as he'd suspected. When he'd finally left the office, *#RunLucieRun* had been trending all over social media. When he'd finally left the office he'd had to fight his way through a media scrum.

His hope that Lydia would spring out to greet him with a smile on her face came to nothing too. He found her in the main living room curled up on a sofa doing something on her phone. She lifted her face at the sound of his footsteps and raised a smile but didn't raise her body. 'How did it go?' she asked.

He pulled a face and threw his suit jacket and tie on the nearest chair. 'A contract we were days away from signing off on and which I'd planned to trumpet in the press as a sign that Tsaliki Shipping is still going from strength to strength, has been withdrawn. I've heard on the grapevine that another of our contracts which is up for renewal at the end of the year is in danger—the owners are in secret talks with one of our competitors.'

'That's worrying.'

He nodded. Lydia had grown up steeped in the business and knew how it worked.

After pouring himself a brandy, he slumped on a seat close to her and looked at her more closely. She looked tired and withdrawn, as if she too were carrying the weight of the world on her shoulders. 'You've been in touch with your family?'

She bit into her bottom lip and nodded.

'So you know?'

'About the shareholder meeting?'

He took a slow sip of his drink and inclined his head. Antoniadis Shipping's major investors were demanding a meeting with Thanasis. Antoniadis Shipping were expecting a new fleet of container ships within the next week. Allegedly, billions still needed to be paid. If those investors pulled their money Antoniadis Shipping would be sunk for good.

She opened her mouth to answer but then her phone buzzed in her hand. She looked at the screen and closed her eyes.

'Not going to answer it?'

'I can't speak to him.'

'Your brother?' he guessed.

Her jaw tightened as she took a long breath. 'It was hard enough talking to my mother. Thanasis is in pieces. I saw a paparazzi picture of him earlier.' She laughed morosely. 'He looks a wreck. I used to think he was the best person in the world and the strongest, and now I'm completely torn. A part of me thinks he deserves all this for the unconscionable way he treated Lucie and then I hate myself for thinking that because the fallout is destroying so many lives. I think it must be destroying him the most because he fell in love with her and now he's lost her and is losing everything else. I've already betrayed my family by sleeping with you and now I'm married to you and carrying your child and so he's lost me too and it feels like I'm leaving him all alone. I don't know how I can speak to him or even what I can say that won't make everything worse for him and for myself because every word I do say will be tainted by lies.' Her stare suddenly landed on his, her eyes flashing. 'And God knows there have been enough lies, by *everyone*.'

Alexis absorbed all this, absorbing too Lydia's unspoken but implicit condemnation of himself for his role in all this. Their fathers' war had started decades ago, before any of their children had been born, but it had been left to the children to be the grown-ups in the room and attempt to repair the wreckage. Their attempts had only blown a fresh bomb on what had already been a vast detonation.

'In hindsight, I would do some things differently,' he acknowledged. He would do everything differently. 'In our defence, once Rebecca had planted the seed of the lie, it seemed the most logical thing to play along with it precisely to prevent the destruction everyone is now living through.' Lucie's own mother had started the lie that Lucie and Thanasis had fallen in love.

'Not you though. You're insulated.' Her smile was

grim. 'You're the only one of us all who is going to get through this whole mess unscathed.'

'You forget that though I'm the one with the least to lose, I'm the one who fought the hardest to stop this all from happening.' He drained his brandy and fixed her with a hard stare. While he appreciated Lydia was upset at everything that was happening to her family, he did not appreciate her attempts to make him the scapegoat for it. 'Do not forget, marriage between our families was my idea and it was a damn good one—your brother was the one who screwed it up, no one else. He drove Lucie away the first time by behaving like an arsehole to her and then drove her away a second time by discovering his conscience.'

'At least he has one,' she bit out pointedly.

He studied her through narrowed eyes wondering when the Lydia who'd been determined to fight any good feeling towards him had made a return. 'What's wrong?'

'Apart from my whole life being destroyed? Nothing.'

'Your *nothing* feels very personal. Have I done something to upset you?'

She eyeballed him back with a loathing he hadn't seen since they'd become lovers and then all the air seemed to puff out of her as she sagged in her seat and hung her head. 'I'm sorry,' she muttered. 'I'm feeling very guilty and emotional today and I'm taking it out on you.'

'Are you sure that's all it is?'

She rubbed her face and nodded.

Crossing to her, he sank onto his knees and smoothed her hair off her wan face. 'You look tired,' he said softly. 'How about I run you a bath? Have a long soak before dinner.'

Something agonised flashed over her beautiful face before she dragged up a small smile. 'How can you be nice to me when I've just been all bitchy and mean to you?'

'I've had worse thrown at me.' Instead of this bringing a proper smile to her face, the smile she had formed fell and her eyes closed. 'Lydia, you're pregnant, your family is being destroyed and your whole world is changing. It is understandable that you're on edge.'

She opened her eyes.

He traced a thumb over her cheekbone. 'I cannot perform miracles but, whatever happens, I promise I will not let your family fall into poverty.'

A line creased her forehead. 'Why would you promise that?'

'Because whether they like it or not, their daughter is my wife and they are my child's grandparents, and that makes them my family too.'

Lydia stayed in the bath so long her fingers and toes turned into prunes. Two nights of passionate sex had released so many endorphins or whatever the chemical was that she'd basically stopped thinking with her brain and, having tried valiantly not to think too much in Alexis's absence that day, her thoughts about him now refused to stay tucked away and had returned with a vengeance. And her fears.

This was her life now. What she'd agreed to. She couldn't start acting like Queen Bitch just because Alexis had recently taken a lover and fallen hard enough to consider marrying her. Whoever the elusive lady was, he hadn't gone through with it, not only because he'd married Lydia, which he couldn't have done if married to someone else, but because he'd had flings with at least three other women in the last month, and those were just the ones she'd read about. He'd probably been cock-struck, a term she remembered from her university days when one of the biggest campus players had fallen hard for one of her friends. In the short time they were together, Maya—yes, another Maya—could have asked him to shave all his hair off and he would have slavishly obeyed. Two weeks later he'd come out of his stupor and dumped her. Lydia wished she could tell herself that she was suffering from the female equivalent.

Going to bed with Alexis had been madness but it had been a madness she'd fully embraced and refused to regret. He'd fully lived up to his reputation and more, and she'd walked away on her own terms. Now she got to live that exquisite joy every night and she had no right to feel jealousy at some poor woman whose heart he'd inevitably broken or feel something a lot like rage-fuelled sickness to imagine the next woman whose heart he'd break. She needed to be concentrating on keeping her own future heartbreak to a minimum. She was no longer confident that when Alexis did take a lover she would be automatically cast aside, was feeling increasingly certain that she really would have to emulate Rebecca Tsaliki's insouciance and turn a blind eye and pretend every minute that his infidelity didn't hurt.

The next day passed for Lydia much like her first full day. She'd seamlessly imported all her files and apps and contacts from her old computers to the new ones but, again, couldn't find the head space to concentrate on her work, couldn't even find the motivation to pitch for the new contracts that had popped up on the networking site in the last few days. She couldn't shift the sickness in her stomach. If she didn't know it was all being caused by stress she'd think morning sickness had decided to throw itself at her just as the pregnancy progressed beyond the first trimester.

Restless, bored with being cooped up and not wanting to wallow in self-pity when she had nothing to be self-pitying about considering that, whatever happened, her child's future was secure just as she'd so wanted, she wandered out of the office Alexis had had created for her. Soon, she found herself studying the pop art hanging on his walls. Such fresh, fun pieces ranging from comically sexy to comically absurd and all brought a much-needed smile to her face.

Moving downstairs, she continued studying them. They suited the man who'd bought them and it made her heart pang to think of him fighting fires to save a business he didn't even want for the sake of his father and siblings. The businesses he did own and from which he'd made his personal fortune were all in hospitality, an industry that suited him much better than shipping, which to Lydia was the least exciting industry going. He even made suits sexy, which she'd never thought she'd find herself thinking. Suits, she'd always believed, were for serious-minded and dare she say boring men like her father and brother, and it had been this association that had actively seen her choose arty, poetic men as her partners; men who wouldn't know one end of a tie from the other and who considered reciting sonnets as romantic and the creation of pop art as frivolous. In her quest to not wake up married to a version of her father or brother, for whom the business was everything, she'd inadvertently found herself with men for whom themselves was everything.

Alexis was everything those men were not and far removed from her father and brother. He wouldn't know one end of a sonnet from another but he had a sense of humour and a zest for life which, combined with his drop-dead gorgeous looks and sexiness, made him irresistible.

But the man who found the shipping industry as exciting as she did was having to delegate the running of his own business to staff so he could concentrate his forensic mind on saving his father's business from the bankruptcy Antoniadis Shipping was headed for. In just two days, Lydia's brother would sit in his boardroom with his main investors knowing it would likely be for the final time.

Shockingly, despite all the bad blood between their

two families, Alexis had promised not to let her family fall into poverty. More shockingly, she believed him. What she didn't believe for a second was that her family would accept his help. Her mother, she knew, would rather starve.

On impulse, she pulled her phone out of her back pocket and was a fingerprint away from calling him when she stopped herself. Alexis was working; fighting the fires that he'd never started even if he had stoked the flames…

Damn it, what had she been doing eulogising him? Yes, he had good traits, many of them, but she didn't need to reinforce them to herself in some kind of daydream like some kind of moon-eyed teenager with a crush. At this rate she'd talk herself into falling in love with him!

'You look like you're arguing with yourself.'

A small scream flew from her mouth as she whipped around and found Alexis standing at the doorway of the dining room where she'd been absently studying a wacky painting of an iconic sixties actress with a cigarette holder in her mouth, the limited palette all fluorescent colours. 'What are you doing home?'

'I live here.' His lips quirked at the corners. 'I had a few hours free of meetings and thought I would join my wife who is suffering from cabin fever for lunch.'

'Lunch?' Where had the morning gone?

His lips quirked again. 'You know. Food.'

God, he was gorgeous, she thought. Just look at him in that dark green suit and with his black hair sticking up on end from all the times he must have run his fingers through it. Alexis was a walking stick of testosterone and to look at him was to make her pulses soar.

Barely aware of her legs moving, Lydia crossed the room, grabbed hold of his tie and yanked him into the room. Pointing to a chair, she barked, 'Sit,' and then firmly shut the door.

The one rule she'd learned in her short time living with Alexis was that when a door was closed it meant the staff were not to enter. She would not let herself think why that was... Actually, she *would* let herself think it. Alexis liked his privacy for sex, and at the moment *she* was his willing partner for sex because she was there and he wanted her, and now he was here and goddammit she wanted him and she didn't have to be in love with him for that. She was just as capable of separating sex from emotions as he was.

'Is this position to your liking?' he asked, seductive bemusement lacing his voice. He'd pulled a dining chair out and placed it against the wall.

'Yes. Now, take your jacket and tie off, and sit.'

He obeyed and then, his eyes alive with sensual anticipation, summoned her with a crook of his finger.

Ignoring his directive, she lifted her top off and chucked it on the floor, stepped out of her sandals and then undid her jeans and pulled them down before stepping out of them too. She made no effort at turning her undressing into a strip show for him but from the expression on Alexis's face, the effect would have been the same, and a giddy sense of power flowed into the hot blood rushing through her.

When Alexis had made the impulsive decision to return to his apartment for lunch, something he'd never done before in the whole of his working life, he'd had dreams of seducing Lydia into the bedroom, of working out all his stress by losing himself in his beautiful wife and her beautiful body. Not once had he imagined this kind of reception and damn if it wasn't as sexy as hell. *She* was as sexy as hell, and now she was prowling across the floor to him wearing only her white lace underwear and with a determined, lascivious glow in her eyes, and it was like he'd woken to find himself in the middle of an erotic fantasy.

When she reached him, she sank straight to her knees and deftly unbuttoned his shirt before reaching for the button and zip of his trousers. Without any ceremony whatsoever she undid them and then tugged them down with his underwear to his hips. A quick lift of his buttocks enabled her to pull them down past an erection that had gone from zero to sixty in seconds, and down to his ankles where she pulled them off and threw them to one side.

And then her lascivious stare landed back on him.

Cheeks heightened with colour, her breathing heavy, she parted his thighs without saying a word, then positioned herself between them and made a fist around his arousal.

His eyes widened at the rush of adrenaline that shot through him.

Still not speaking with anything but her bright, lust-filled eyes, she began to masturbate him, her fist moving up and down his length, slapping his hand away when he reached for a breast.

'Lydia...' *Theos*, that thick voice was his.

With one hand now pressed firmly on his chest to keep him still, she bent her head and took him into her hot mouth.

Submitting to her will and the exquisite sensation of what she was doing to him, Alexis groaned loudly and rested his head back against the wall.

Slavishly she made love to him with her mouth and hand, erotic pleasure thrumming through his every cell...

She cupped his balls.

'God, Lydia...' Her name on his lips morphed into another groan.

Tighter the pads of her fingers pressed into his chest, tighter her hold on his arousal, her movements increasing, and when he raised his head and saw her beautiful blonde head bobbing up and down on his lap, the telltale tugging of his loins was almost more than he could control.

As if she sensed he was on the brink of coming, she pulled her lips up his erection one long last time and then she was on her feet, freeing her breasts from her bra and yanking her knickers down her legs and kicking them away...and then she was straddling his lap.

Clasping his cheeks in her hands, she gazed into his eyes with an intensity he'd never seen in the hazel before, and with a loud moan of pleasure sank down on his length.

Theos, she was more than ready for him.

With only a fleeting kiss to his lips, she dragged her fingers to the back of his head and pulled his face down to her breasts. It was the only control she ceded to him and he took complete advantage, sucking one then the other in the way that drove her so wild. She'd barely started riding him when he felt her thicken around him and then she arched her neck and ground herself down, holding his head tightly to keep his mouth at her breast as she convulsed around him.

It was the most beautiful, perfect moment of his life, and he savoured it, letting her take every ounce of her pleasure before grabbing hold of her hips and thrusting himself hard up into her, his own climax coming in quick succession as he spurted his seed deep inside her and their mouths finally fused as the last of their orgasms ripped through them.

Lydia couldn't catch her breath. Couldn't think. No, was *afraid* to think. The beats of her heart weren't just racing from the thrilling power of what they'd just shared but from fear.

Where had that sensual, demanding woman come from? She'd only met her once, her weekend with Alexis, when she'd been completely unafraid and had made love to him with the same intensity that he'd made love to her. The very fact that she'd been so unafraid that night proved she should have been terrified, and now she was afraid to unwrap her arms from around his neck or move her cheek from his, terrified of what he'd find in her eyes. More terrified of what she wouldn't find in his.

Whatever point she'd been trying to make to herself had backfired, and she had to plead with herself to keep it together, to remind herself that when her skin was no longer pressed to Alexis's and the heavy beats of his heart were no longer dancing with the beats of hers and he was no longer inside her, this rush would pass and all these emotions that had sprung up from nowhere would go back to the nowhere from where they came.

She wasn't falling in love with him. She wasn't. It was just a chemical rush.

Mercies came in unexpected places and hers came from the ringing of a phone.

'That's yours,' she said, climbing off his lap and grabbing his discarded suit jacket where the ringing was coming from and passing it to him, then used the excuse of gathering the rest of their discarded clothes to avoid eye contact a little bit longer, using that fragment of time to pull herself together.

Whoever was calling, he didn't answer. Nor did he mention who the caller had been. The tightness of his mouth, though, told her whoever had called had been unwanted.

He'd just finished tucking his shirt in when his phone buzzed with a message.

Lydia, having pulled her top back over her head, saw

the fresh tightening of his lips at whatever was on his screen. 'What's wrong?'

'Nothing.' The way he said it made her stomach plummet and when she recognised the phone, it plummeted some more. Alexis had two phones, one that was strictly for business and one that was friends and family. It was his personal phone in his hand.

'I thought that was my stock answer,' she chided lightly. 'Is it something or someone important?'

The blue-grey eyes fixed onto hers with a gravity she couldn't remember seeing in them before. 'If I tell you, it will hurt you.'

Alarm shot through her veins. 'Is it about my family?'

His expression didn't change. 'No.'

Now her blood pressure plummeted too. Or did it rise? She didn't know, knew only that she felt suddenly light-headed, and not in a good way.

With his *no* hanging between them, poisoning the air she breathed, she somehow managed to hold onto the airiness of her tone. 'Shouldn't you reply to it?'

Grimness crept into his voice. 'No.'

'It's bad manners to leave a lover hanging.' She slipped her feet into her sandals and added, 'Not to mention cruel.'

The tightening of his lips and the flickering in his eyes told her she'd hit bullseye. Smiling to show she didn't care, Lydia strode to the door. 'Call and put her out of her misery. I'll order lunch for us.'

The gravity in his expression didn't change. 'It was over long ago.'

She shrugged and gave another bright smile. 'Then deal with it however you see fit. Just remember she's a human with feelings.'

Only after she'd popped into the kitchen to order food for them did Lydia lock herself in a bathroom and throw up what remained of her breakfast.

CHAPTER TEN

ALEXIS STUDIED LYDIA discreetly but thoroughly as they shared their evening meal on the roof terrace. The humidity had lessened a little, the blazing heat of the day now a bearable warmth, and she'd changed out of her faithful jeans to sit out in it, wearing a simple cream skirt and silver scooped top. The silky hair he adored loose had been tied into an elegant knot and she must have trimmed her fringe because she hadn't spent half the evening blowing it out of her eyes.

Watching her gracefully fork succulent slow-cooked lamb into her succulent mouth made his chest tighten.

'You're beautiful,' he murmured, almost without thinking.

She gave a narrow-eyed smile. 'What brought that on?'

He raised a shoulder. 'Just making an observation. Did you speak to your mother?' Lydia had said before he'd returned to the office that she was going to call her.

She nodded 'She's expecting me home on Sunday.'

Sunday. The date they would tell their families and then the world about their marriage.

The small amount of light in her eyes dimmed. 'She thinks I'm coming home. She doesn't know I'm only coming back to stick the boot even harder into them.'

'What are you going to say to them?'

'I don't know.' Gazing into the distance, she said, 'I keep thinking about what I can say that will stop them hating me or at the least stop them hating our child.' Her stare landed back on him. 'Mum already thinks Lucie used witchcraft to cast a spell on Thanasis. It's a long shot but she might just believe you used your Lucifer powers to trick me into your bed and into a marriage.'

'Even though marriage was your idea and you said your vows under your own free will?' he said steadily.

'She doesn't need to know that.'

'Doesn't she?'

'It would be the most unforgivable thing I could do. You know this.'

'Even though I am prepared to lay it straight with my family and tell them to accept you or else?'

'It's different for you.'

'How?'

'You hold the purse strings.'

'I would still demand they accept you and our marriage even if I had no financial hold over them.'

'My family will never accept you and never accept our marriage. If I'm lucky, they'll let me and the baby through their door one day in the future but never you.'

'And you won't fight to make them accept me?'

She laughed morosely. 'There would be no point. In their eyes, you're Lucifer.'

And Lydia would never try to convince them otherwise.

Taking a deep breath to smother the acidic bile rising in his throat, Alexis said, 'You know, there is still a chance your brother can pull a rabbit out of the hat and convince the investors to hold tight. It doesn't have to be over for Antoniadis Shipping.' He gave a tight smile. 'If the miracle does happen then your family might be more amenable to accepting me.'

Her laugh almost sounded convincing. 'Not even Jesus could perform such a miracle.'

'A lot can happen in two days,' he pointed out.

'Two sleeps but only one full day,' she pointed out back before stabbing at some roasted butternut squash and dipping it into the feta and yogurt mousse.

'I'm just saying don't convince yourself it's game over. Your brother has all the skills and acumen to turn it round.'

'I know he does. It's whether he has the will that's in question. But let's not talk about my family any more otherwise I'll cry and this delicious food doesn't need extra seasoning. How are things going for Tsaliki Shipping? Do you think you've stabilised things yet?'

He shook his head and took a drink of his red wine, which did nothing to smother the bitter taste on his tongue. 'No. The story about us forcing Lucie to marry Thanasis refuses to die and I don't see how it will if she doesn't come out of hiding and officially deny it.'

'You wouldn't ask her to do that, would you?'

He took a long breath. If up to him he wouldn't just ask Lucie, he'd force her, but he kept his private thoughts to himself. His wife had proved very protective and defensive of his stepsister and he didn't want to fall into an argument, not when he was already trying to rid himself of the bitterness that had risen in him at her refusal to even consider fighting for her family to accept him. 'No. But I would hope she did it of her own volition.'

She pulled a rueful face. 'I'm afraid that's as likely to happen as my mother not disowning me. Lucie gave up her job and her home to marry Thanasis for your family's sake, and she was repaid with lies. She doesn't owe any of you or any of us anything.'

He eyed her meditatively and swallowed back fresh bitterness. 'You make it sound like we're still in opposing camps.'

'I'm still an Antoniadis and always will be.'

'But married to a Tsaliki and always will be,' he reminded her, and then took another deep inhale to smother the agitation simmering in his guts. 'For all that things are yet to stabilise, I remain confident that I can still turn things round with Tsaliki Shipping. Do you know of Hans Dreyman?'

'The name's familiar but I can't think where from.'

'Dreyman Co, the German food manufacturer, one of the top food manufacturers in the world. Their products are sold all over the world. You'll know many of their brand names. We've been transporting their goods for years.'

'Is this the contract you heard on the grapevine is threatening to look elsewhere?'

He shook his head and grimly said, 'No, that's a different company. Hans, though, has a lot of influence in the corporate world and if I can get him to lend us his support and endorse us, it will go a long way to calming nerves. I learned today that he's travelling into Athens tomorrow and that on Friday night he's going to Theo Nikolaidis's summer party—I too have an invitation to that party.'

'Then you have to go.'

'Yes. The question is do you want to come with me?'

'I don't know Theo but I know his wife, Helena,' she said slowly. 'She's discreet but we have mutual friends. If I come with you then there's a good chance the whole of Athens will know about us before we've finished our first canapé.'

'It will get you out of the apartment and it might work as a distraction to the news that will have come out about the resolution of the meeting between your brother and his investors.'

'As much as I'd love to go, you know I can't do that to my family—it would be too cruel. Friday is going to be intolerable for them. I can't add to it. We need to stick to the agreed timeline, and you'll just have to go to the party without me.'

'As long as I have your blessing.'

Surprise flashed in her eyes. 'You don't need my blessing to do anything.'

'I don't need it but I do want it.'

'Then fine, you have my blessing to go to the party without me.' Before he could breathe a little easier at this—Friday, he knew, was going to be especially hard for her and she'd be spending the majority of it on her own—she drained her grape juice and jauntily added, 'If you don't want to go alone you must have dozens of names stored in your personal phone who would jump at the chance to be your plus one for the night.'

Working hard to stop the edge creeping back into his voice, he said, 'The only name that's ever been in my phone that I would even consider taking in your place is my sister, Athena, but as she's liable to spend the evening flirting with any man with a pulse and decent bank balance and making snide comments about all the other guests, I'll give her a miss and go to the party on my own.'

She stilled, just a fleeting stillness in which a whole host of emotions flashed in her eyes, but he saw it and the edge subsided. He mustn't forget that while they were both navigating their new life together, Lydia didn't just have her family's destruction hanging over her along with the real possibility of losing her family, but was pregnant too. He shouldn't be adding pressure to her or allowing bitterness to set in over things that were yet to happen.

'One party you won't have to miss is the one I'm hosting next Friday at the nightclub. It's for a friend's birthday, and you *will* be coming with me for it.'

Her smile looked forced. 'I'm not a nightclub kind of girl, remember?'

He looked her up and down, the silver of her top reminding him of the dress she'd worn their first night together. 'I don't know,' he murmured. 'You seemed to enjoy yourself at my club the last time you were there.'

Lydia was lying on her side, Alexis spooned against her, his hand making slow circles over her belly. She couldn't settle her brain. When Alexis had come home from work they'd taken a swim in the roof terrace pool together and played three games of backgammon before getting an early night that had turned into a long night of lovemaking, but she was still too jittery over what tomorrow would bring to switch mind or body off.

'You never did tell me why you turned those marriage proposals down,' he said sleepily.

Her eyes opened. 'You already know the answer,' she whispered. 'I didn't love them enough.'

Didn't love them enough because in her yearning for something different, she'd gone for arty men too absorbed with themselves and their artistic creations to fall in love with, men she'd never had to cut the safety nets for. Never even wanted to. She'd refused to entertain even living with them. She'd wanted to escape the 'men in suits' who filled her life, wanted something different for herself than the life her mother had made, but had never found the courage to fully go out there and get it.

'But you did love them?'

Her heart swelled and then tightened, and she had to swallow a compression in her throat to answer. 'I don't know. I thought I did...or maybe I just told myself I did. Maybe you were right when you said I'm a commitment-phobe like you.'

'No,' he corrected quietly. 'I said you were the one afraid of commitment, not me.'

'Alexis, I'm twenty-seven years old and you're only the third man I've been with, whereas you've been with…' She swallowed, unable to voice a number that didn't make her stomach twist.

'I've been with a lot of women,' he supplied into the silence.

'And how many of those women have been more than a fling?' For all that she'd valiantly tried to block her thoughts from returning to the call and message that had come through on Alexis's personal phone after they'd made love in the dining room, Lydia's mind now filled with the myriad women she'd seen pictured on his arm. Nausea filled her twisted stomach. Which one of those women had been the one to try to reach him that day? Had she been the woman he'd wanted to marry?

'Not many,' he confessed.

It took a long beat before she could force herself to ask, 'And of those, how many have you even contemplated a proper relationship with?'

He took a deep, long inhale as if bracing himself before saying, his voice heavy, 'Just one.'

A sharper, hotter twist in her stomach and a deeper roll of nausea stopped her probing any further.

He tightened his hold around her and kissed the top of her head. 'I made my vows to *you*, my angel. Never forget that.'

* * *

Friday morning arrived and with it a sickness in Lydia's stomach far worse than any other.

In a few short hours the shareholders' meeting would commence. Unless a miracle occurred then in a few short hours Antoniadis Shipping would cease to exist.

She waited until Alexis left for another day of fighting fires in his office before getting out of bed.

She'd been cooped up for long enough. She needed to get out into the fresh air, proper fresh air, now, before the sun rose higher and the temperatures soared.

All too aware of the press and members of the public with nothing better to do than stalk Alexis's apartment block with the cameras of their phones primed, she threw her running clothes and trainers on, shoved her hair under the brown wig, filled her bottle with fresh water, donned her running shades, and sneaked out through the apartment block's car park.

Minutes later she was entering the metro, only one stop away from the one she took from her family home, with early-bird tourists and the day's workers, emerging back into the morning light a short while later at the Acropolis stop. She didn't receive a second glance from anyone. Instead of turning right with the tourists, she turned left and joined the Dionysiou Areopagitou walkway. Just past the church of St Demetrius she disappeared through the trees onto a wonderfully shaded and cool running route, pounding the familiar path to the old quarry, paying no attention as she passed it nor any attention to the solo rock climber already scaling the crag further along, no attention to anything at all, not even when she took the landscaped walk up to the top of the hill.

Only when she reached the marble Philopappos Monument did she stop to drink some water and take a breath. A couple of tourists of around her parents' age had already reached the hill's summit and, though she couldn't understand the language they were speaking, she knew they were raving at the spectacular view of the Acropolis. Just as she was wondering if they'd yet found the wooden observatory from where it felt like you could reach out and touch the Parthenon, the woman held her phone out to Lydia and made the universal sign of taking a photo.

Sticking her thumb up to show she understood, she took the phone and as she lifted it to get them and the Acropolis into frame, the couple put their arms around each other and pressed their cheeks together, beaming grins alive on their faces. A pang of melancholy tightened her chest at their obvious happiness, a pang that grew when they headed off on the path she'd just run with their hands clasped together. Her parents were still like that with each other.

Theirs was a future she would never have. Not with Alexis.

Wiping away a tear that had fallen from nowhere, she drank some more water and set back off to finish the trail.

For all the good the run had done her physically, emotionally Lydia felt worse. The tenterhooks she was hanging on were bleeding her heart. She couldn't stop checking her phone for updates of the meeting, and by the time lunch had passed, the only news to have come out was that the investors had left soon after they'd arrived. No press release was, as yet, expected.

As for her brother, there had been no word. Neither of her parents had heard from him.

Selfishly—and Lydia hated herself for the selfishness of her thoughts and emotions—it was the evening's party making her feel so sick. This was a society event that would be packed with the rich and beautiful. There would be women there who'd shared Alexis's bed. What if one of those women was the one he'd thought about marrying, the one woman he'd contemplated a real relationship with? As hard as she tried, Lydia just could not stop herself thinking about her, couldn't stop herself trawling the Internet for all the women he'd been linked with since their night together. Which one was she? And then she'd wondered if maybe the woman had come before her and that Alexis had cheated on her with Lydia. And then she'd wondered why she was doing this, why she couldn't just do as she'd promised herself and make the most of what she had with Alexis while she had it because, while she had him, Alexis was everything a woman could dream of in a man and in a husband.

She thought back to the night they'd agreed their terms of marriage and his mocking smile as he'd said, *'No demands that I be faithful?'*

'I wouldn't waste my breath.'

What if she *had* wasted it? Would she still be facing a future that sat in her chest like the weight of doom? And what if...?

What if she were to ask it of him now? What if she were to lay her heart on the line and admit the thought of him with another woman made her feel physically sick? He wouldn't laugh at her, that much she knew. He would take her seriously, but that didn't mean he would give her the answer she craved. For heaven's sake, she shouldn't even be craving it! She'd known what she was agreeing to when she'd agreed to this marriage, and torturing herself like this was only going to make her ill and she couldn't allow that to happen, especially not with her precious baby to think of.

Her next call to her mother went to voicemail.

Needing to be alone, she went up to the bedroom and curled into one of the sofas, hugging the phone to her chest. For the first time since she'd gone to her first childhood sleepover, she felt a keening ache for her fierce, determined, loving mother, but the one thing she felt so in desperate need of comfort for was the one thing she couldn't yet tell her about and would be the thing that drove them apart.

Maybe she should go to the house and sit with them while they waited for news...but how to explain that she was magically back in Athens? She'd been so grateful that with everything going on her parents had been too distracted to question her about what she'd been getting up to. She hadn't had to lie to them since the initial lie that she was going to England.

How was she going to cope without her family? She didn't know how she could, but she had no choice. Would have no choice. Could only pray their anger with her didn't last for ever because certainty was growing that she was going to need them.

By the time Alexis came home it felt like she was close to breaking. How could there be no news? How was she going to endure Alexis spending the evening in the presence of ex-lovers and probable future lovers? Who was to say he'd even come home to her after the party?

The bedroom door opened.

She jumped to her feet. 'Have you heard anything?'

'Only rumours,' he said heavily as he threw his suit jacket and tie onto the nearest surface, one of his habits she was already becoming accustomed to. Crossing the room to her, he wrapped her in his arms and rested his chin on the top of her head.

Neither of them spoke for the longest time, and as the seconds passed and Lydia's lungs filled with his divine scent and the beat of his heart thrummed steadily against her, a little of her angst loosened. Alexis would never know how comforting his embrace was to her and how safe it made her feel, even if that comfort and safety were dangerous wishful thinking delusions of her own mind.

'I don't know what happened in the meeting,' he eventually said, 'but the one solid piece of news I received from a reliable source is that Lucie was seen entering the Antoniadis building shortly after the meeting started.'

Lydia reared her head back so she could look up at him. 'She's back?'

'Yes, but whether it's for good or ill, I don't know. Nothing has been seen of her or your brother since.'

Closing her eyes, she rested her face back into the crook of his neck.

He massaged the back of her neck. 'I don't have to go tonight. I can stay here with you.'

'You have to go.'

'I don't.'

'You do.' Touched beyond belief that he would even consider missing the party for her sake when it was so important that he go, she looked back up at him and smiled wanly. 'Antoniadis Shipping is probably over but you can still save Tsaliki Shipping from the same fate. Both of our fathers' legacies don't have to be destroyed.'

'Lydia...'

Her heart skipped at his tone and the intensity in his blue-grey eyes pierced straight into her veins, and then whatever he'd been about to say to her was forgotten as his hungry mouth found hers. In moments he had her against the wall, all their restrictive items of clothing ripped off, and he was inside her, her arms tight around his neck and their mouths fused together as, for a few heady minutes, they both forgot everything except each other.

After making love again for a much, much longer time, Alexis went for his shower. Alone in the bed, Lydia checked her phone and sighed. Nothing.

She felt better in herself though. How could she fear Alexis would already be looking for a lover when the chemistry between them blazed so strong?

She must have dozed off for the next time she opened her eyes, he was leaning over her, fully dressed in an embroidered blue suit with matching waistcoat but no tie, and smelling so fresh and divine that she grabbed the back of his neck to haul him closer, just so she could bury her nose into his neck and inhale him.

Laughing, he buried his nose into her neck before his mouth found hers and he kissed her with a savage possessiveness that left her breathless with longing.

Eyes gleaming, he gave her one more kiss before moving away and then pointed down to his crotch. 'Look what you've done.'

She grinned and sat up, deliberately letting the sheets fall down to expose her breasts. And then, to tease him some more, deliberately cupped one breast while dipping her other hand between her legs.

He was back on the bed before she had time to blink.

CHAPTER ELEVEN

AFTER TAKING A shower and having something to eat, Lydia sat in bed stalking her phone. When Alexis had finally left for the party it was with a promise not to be too late and with the order that she be waiting in bed naked for him, an order she was more than happy to obey. It was also with the promise that if he heard anything about her brother, he would call her, a promise she'd made in turn.

Putting her phone to one side, she gazed up at the ceiling. She had to stop worrying about the future. It would happen when it happened. For now, Alexis was hers and she was his…

Her phone rang.

She snatched it up. It was her mother.

Once the call ended she sat for a long time in a fugue trying to process everything. She needed to call Alexis but as she put her thumb back to her phone, a massive burst of euphoria wrenched through her and suddenly she didn't want to speak to him, she wanted to see him, *needed* to see him, right now.

Leaning over to the bedside table, she pressed the intercom.

'Can you arrange for a car for me, please?' she said quickly. 'I'll be ready to leave in ten minutes.'

Call done, she bounced off the bed and raced into her dressing room. Throwing on underwear first, she chose a taupe dress she'd bought on a whim because she liked the colour but had never worn. Mid-thigh-length, it wrapped around the neck halter-fashion but draped so cleverly over the breasts and belly that no one who knew her would suspect she was pregnant. A vigorous brush of her hair, a sweep of mascara, blush and lip gloss and she was good to go...until she was halfway down the stairs and realised she was barefoot. Luckily she still had the sparkling silver sandals she'd bought for the wedding, and she slipped her feet into them, enjoying the elevated height they gave her.

Feeling like she could fly, she climbed into the back of the waiting car and told the driver to take her the short drive to Alexis.

The Nikolaidises' home was classical Greek architecture at its finest, and when Lydia got out of the car she imagined senators from ancient times passing through the marble pillars flanking the entrance.

Helena Nikolaidis was at the door to greet her—without an official invitation Lydia had given her name to the security guards at the bottom of the drive who'd only taken her seriously because she was an Antoniadis and the fact she was being driven in a chauffeured car.

'Forgive me for gatecrashing,' Lydia said after they'd exchanged kisses, 'but I'm here to see Alexis Tsaliki.'

Helena arched an eyebrow in surprise then quickly composed herself. 'You are more than welcome,' she assured her, although she was clearly itching to ask why Lydia would be seeking her family's enemy. 'Let me show you around and see if we can find Alexis—I can't remember where I last saw him.'

Inside, the home was of a free-flowing semi-open-plan design with wide sliding doors separating the plentiful rooms, central to it all a stunning white marble circular staircase. There was a real buzz in the air, champagne and canapés flowing, the music playing loud enough to dance to but low enough to still make conversation. People, hundreds of them all clothed in beautiful dresses and tailored suits, were mingling all over the place, some in small huddles where it looked like they were exchanging state secrets and others in larger groups where they were clearly just enjoying each other's company.

One of the waiting staff approached Helena and whispered something in her ear.

'Excuse me,' Helena said to Lydia. 'There's something I need to attend to. I won't be long.'

'Don't worry about me,' Lydia assured her. 'I'll find him.'

Alexis was so tall he should have been easy to spot, but after scanning all the faces on the ground floor, trying to blend in and be unobtrusive so as not to catch the attention of anyone who knew her, she'd seen no sight of him. A small group of guests, though, were climbing the wide stairs from the basement, and, seeing another guest descend them, she decided to follow suit.

The basement was a vast, open space that covered the whole footprint of the house with artfully decorated pillars structurally supporting it running across its centre. She saw two snooker tables in one section, gambling tables, a large fully stocked bar manned by three staff, comfortable sofas, caught a peek of a home cinema behind velvet curtains, but no Alexis. Ready to cut back across the basement and go up and explore the gardens, she suddenly glimpsed a couple leaning against one of the pillars. Or, rather, the man wearing the navy embroidered suit and holding a glass of champagne was leaning back against it. The woman, taller, blonder and more beautiful than Lydia, was leaning into him, their torsos a feather away from touching, coquettish delight alive on her face. Laughing, she put her hands around his neck, pressed her breasts into his chest and leaned in for a kiss.

Lydia's chest turned to ice.

How the hell had he allowed himself to become trapped? Alexis wondered. He still hadn't spoken to Hans, and now Angeliki Poulis, an old flame, had made a beeline for him and was under the impression that he wanted to hear every last detail about her recent trip to Marrakech and that he would find every last detail as scintillating as she believed it to be.

Refusing to respond in kind to her flirtatious smiles

and giggles, he simply waited with barely concealed impatience for her to stop talking so he could extract himself without having to cause a scene. Angeliki was a spoilt daddy's girl who thrived on drama. Alexis didn't want any drama, wanted only to find Hans, have a good talk with him, and then go home to Lydia. But, of course, he couldn't tell Angeliki that. Angeliki had the biggest mouth in Athens.

When she put her hands around his neck and leaned her face closer for a kiss, his patience snapped. Clasping the hands, he was about to pull them off him when the hairs on the nape of his neck lifted.

Turning his head, he saw the small, curvy figure in the taupe dress some distance away, her gaze fixed on him with an expression that could only be described as agonised horror.

The drumming of blood in Alexis's head and disbelief at the apparition before him froze him into place and froze his reactions, and now he was the one watching in horror as Lydia's open mouth closed into a tight line and her beautiful face contorted.

She'd already reached the stairs when he pulled himself out of his stupor.

Disentangling himself from Angeliki like he'd been scalded, he hurried after his wife, taking the stairs three at a time and then taking the quickest, longest strides of his life to catch her as she stepped into the central reception room, overtaking her and then spinning around to block her path.

If it were possible for fire and brimstone to be fired from eyes then he was a damned man.

'That was not what it looked like,' he said immediately and firmly.

She folded her arms across her chest and gave a shrug of contemptuous nonchalance. With a smile so brittle the slightest knock would shatter it, she said, 'It really doesn't matter. I just came here to tell you that Lucie did come back to save Antoniadis Shipping—it appears she's as madly in love with my brother as he is with her. The investors believe she's spent the last week in hospital with a relapse of her head injury. A statement will be issued in the morning about the new date for the wedding. Antoniadis Shipping has been saved and I imagine the knock-on effect will benefit Tsaliki Shipping too. I just thought you'd want to know all that.' Her smile widened. 'Looking at all the guests here, you're going to be spoilt for choice over who to celebrate the hardest with. Enjoy the rest of your night.'

Lydia had barely taken three steps past him when Alexis caught her wrist and spun her back round.

'What the hell, Lydia?' he said tightly, his face dark with anger.

Drawing herself as tall as she could get, knowing the entire fabric of her being was a thread away from unravelling, she hissed, 'Take your hand off me.' And then she snatched her wrist away with such force that she stumbled, would have gone sprawling if he hadn't caught her with one deft hook of his arm.

Before she could pull herself away a second time,

he was frogmarching her through the reception room whilst simultaneously using the hand not trapping her to him to call his driver.

Once outside and away from the prying eyes of the other guests, Lydia pulled herself out of his hold and held tightly to her belly, as if she could protect the growing life from the cauldron of nausea bubbling and broiling inside her, the euphoria of her mother's call all gone.

'What the hell is wrong with you?' he demanded. 'Nothing happened. Nothing was going to happen. I was about to extricate myself from the situation when I saw you standing there.'

'I don't care! I'm not your keeper!'

'If you don't care then why are you shouting and why the hell did you run away?'

'Because it was humiliating!'

Because after the coldness of shock had come the heat...red-hot jealous heat.

She, the woman who'd never experienced an ounce of jealousy in her life, had wanted to fly at that woman with her arms around Alexis and physically drag her off him, and then batter her fists into his chest and scream in his face until he swore he would never look at another woman again.

'*Humiliating?* Angeliki didn't know I was married—no one knew because you insisted we keep it a secret, but do you seriously think I was encouraging her?'

'I don't know!' All Lydia knew was how she'd felt in the moment when all the fears she'd tried so hard to bury had been realised and the future she'd been dread-ing had revealed itself more sharply and painfully than she'd ever allowed herself to imagine.

Oh, God, tears were burning the backs of her eyes, her heart thumping so hard the beats pounded like drums between her ears. She wasn't just close to unravelling, she was close to disintegrating and she needed to get a grip on herself right now.

Large hands clasped her shoulders, his stare boring so hard into her that it compelled her to lift her gaze to the tight fury etched on his handsome face. 'Do you seriously think I would try to hook up with someone else the first minute your back's turned? When we've only been married five minutes?'

'But that's just it, isn't it?' she cried. 'Five minutes or five weeks or five months, we both know it's going to happen, especially when the baby comes!' When she was sore and tired and needing her bed for sleep and only sleep.

If she'd thought his face was etched with fury before, it was nothing on what blazed on it now. Releasing her shoulders to fold his arms around his chest, he said tightly, 'You never fail to assume the worst of me.'

'I'm just being realistic! I do believe you that nothing happed with that woman but I can't help how I feel and we both know it will happen in the future—you're Alexis Tsaliki!' She *did* believe him—Alexis was no liar—but the jealousy and pain that had burned through her...she could still feel its scald in her veins, and it came to her that one day soon, she would feel this pain and it would be for real, and if it hurt like this now then she couldn't even imagine what it would feel like then, when he was burrowed even further into her heart. 'I thought I knew what I was agreeing to and thought I could handle it but I *can't*. I should never have agreed to your terms and I wish like hell that I hadn't. I can't pretend to be like your stepmother, I *can't*!'

It was like the whole of his enormous body flexed. 'What are you saying? Spell it out to me, Lydia.'

'That I want to go home!' she screamed. 'My real home!'

For the longest time he simply stared at her before his features contorted into something almost inhuman. 'Oh, you do, do you?'

She shivered, suddenly frightened, not of him but of something about him, the inhuman contortion that managed to be human enough to make her pounding heart twist.

The car that had so recently dropped her off pulled up before them.

Alexis opened the door, and in a tone cold enough to freeze the sun, said, 'Get in.'

Wishing she could run away, run until her muscles screamed in protest, Lydia got into the car and compressed herself into the door at the far side.

Not a word or look was exchanged between them during the drive back. For the first time ever, Alexis angled away from her... No, that wasn't right. He'd turned away from her the night before they'd married when she'd confessed her reasons for not wanting to tell him about their baby until it had been born.

In silence, they got into the elevator. Powerfully aware of his tightly controlled posture and of the tension emanating from him, Lydia squeezed her eyes shut and concentrated on breathing. She was trembling, every part of her turned to jelly.

He held the door open for her and then strode ahead, removing his suit jacket as he walked and throwing it onto the closest armchair in the living room. 'Take the rest of the night off,' he said curtly to the butler.

When Alexis was growing up, whenever a member of the family had an upset stomach, his father would order a port and brandy to be concocted for them, a medicinal trick he'd picked up on an English business trip. Always as healthy as a horse, Alexis had never needed this concoction but the tight, nauseous feeling in his guts was worsening by the minute and he poured himself a healthy measure of both and drank it in one large swallow. Pouring another, he restrained himself by only drinking half of it.

Only then could he bring himself to look at her.

Leaning against the bar, cradling his glass, he breathed in deeply and contemplated her with an evenness that was at complete odds with the heavy, erratic beats of his heart. He'd never felt the vibrations of his heart through his skin before.

Lydia had perched herself on an armchair. Her face, he noted cynically, was etched with misery.

'So, my angel from Hades, you have decided that you don't want to be married to me after all.'

She flinched. She would never know how fitting his name for her was. His beautiful angel sent from Hades to destroy him.

'Just tell me one thing—was this your plan from the start?'

Her eyes widened, eyebrows drawing together in confusion. Her voice was barely audible. 'Was what my plan?'

'To hope for a miracle with Antoniadis Shipping.'

The throat he'd fooled himself into believing would be his to kiss for ever moved. 'I hoped but I didn't dare believe it would happen.'

'But you did hope for it, and did you plan from the start to leave me if your hope was realised and the company saved?'

'No, of course not.'

He gave a sardonic laugh. 'So you're an opportunist then. I should have known.'

'What are you talking about?'

'Don't treat me like a fool. You only agreed to my terms because you didn't trust that I would always provide for you and the baby without a ring on your finger. The company being saved means your income from the shares is safe and you no longer need me, even if your family do throw you out and disown you.' He gave a tight smile. 'And I am sure you know me well enough by now to know that I will still be a father to our child and provide for it.'

'I have never thought that, not once.'

'Maybe not consciously but your wish to return your

real home tells its own story. Tonight was the perfect storm for you. You have never trusted me and seeing me with Angeliki gave you the out you've wanted from the start—you saw what you wanted to see and jumped at the escape route it opened for you.'

'That's not true!' she protested shakily. 'Not in the way you're making it out to be. I told you already, I do believe you that nothing happened or was going to happen between you, but—'

'But you still saw what you wanted to see—what you *expected* to see—and jumped to the easiest conclusion because all you see me as is a sex-mad Lothario who would cheat on his pregnant wife at the first opportunity.'

'No!'

'*Yes.* In your eyes I'm just Alexis Tsaliki, the commitment-shy Lucifer who can't be trusted to keep his trousers on when a beautiful woman catches his eye.'

'You never promised to be faithful to me.'

'Yes, I did.'

'You did *not*! When I said I wouldn't waste my breath in asking it of you, you *laughed*.'

'"I promise you love, honour and respect; to be *faithful to you*, and not to forsake you until death do us part",' he ground out. 'To be *faithful* to you. I made that promise to you in front of witnesses and God.'

'But you didn't mean it!' she cried. 'You never once said you were going to take our vows seriously.'

'Because I knew you wouldn't believe me—in my world, actions speak louder than words, and I'd hoped, by proving myself a true and faithful husband to you, that you'd learn to trust me and believe in me, but as I've learned with you, I'm damned whatever I do. You don't want to believe in me.'

'I do, of course I do, you're the father of my child, and it's all well and good saying that actions speak louder than words but your track record... You don't *have* a track record! You've never sustained a relationship with a woman in the whole of your adult life! For heaven's sake, Alexis, you were only in a position to marry me in the first place because either you or the woman you came close to committing to got cold feet within weeks.'

'What the hell are you talking about?'

'The woman you were going to marry! The one you made the changes in your bedroom for! That happened weeks and weeks before we married and can only have lasted five minutes because I lost count of the number of women you were pictured with after I left your bed.'

The laughter that followed this landed like nails on a chalkboard to Lydia's ears. Shaking his head, his face twisted in something that could be either a smile or a grimace, he swirled the liquid in his glass before throwing it down his throat, and then he reached for the bottle of brandy, refilled the glass and took another large drink of it.

The smiling grimace was still alive on his face when his eyes next locked onto hers. 'It was you.'

'What was?'

'The woman I was planning to marry. It was you, Lydia. It was always you.'

CHAPTER TWELVE

THE ROOM WAS SPINNING, Alexis's face a sudden blur, the noise in Lydia's head deafening.

'You're drunk,' she whispered uncertainly.

'Not yet, but by the end of this night I hope to be.' He winked, raised his glass to her, and drank half of what remained in it. Wiping his mouth with the back of his hand, he gave another of those awful laughs. 'Did you not listen to me when I said I didn't want to be like my father? Or when I told you on the night we agreed to marry that marriage is not a game to be played with? I've seen too much pain and hurt caused by marriage vows taken in vain to ever play that game. I always knew I would settle down when the woman I could see myself growing old with came into my life, but I wasn't prepared to string women along and ruin lives until I found her.' The ugly smile faded into starkness. 'I found her three months ago.'

Her thumping heart jumped into her throat.

'Something happened between us that weekend, Lydia, and I know you felt it too, and I don't just mean the sex.'

She shrank into herself, remembering the way they'd parted. Remembering, too, how much it had hurt to walk away. 'But...that can't be true...you were horrible and dismissive to me.'

He held her stare. 'Have you never heard of pride?'

Blood was whooshing through her head, a roar of noise that made it impossible to think coherently, impossible to take in what he was saying.

'When you left...' He swore and drained his glass. 'I couldn't get you out of my mind.' He tapped his temple. 'You were in here. Everywhere I went. It was like you'd possessed me. I kept hearing your laughter and smelling your perfume and I knew there was no way I could spend the rest of my life without you in it. That's why I proposed a marriage between our families—the truce was just a smokescreen. I didn't even need it. Tsaliki Shipping had already weathered the worst of the storm of bad publicity.'

'But if you...'

'I proposed a marriage between you and me.'

She shook her head, not in disagreement but in disbelief. 'No. That can't be true.' It had always been Thanasis and Lucie...hadn't it?

'Ask your brother.' That awful, awful laugh rang through her ears again. 'He turned me down flat. Looked at me as if I were the devil reincarnate for even suggesting I marry you. I think that was the point when I really understood why you'd had to walk away from me. That war between our fathers...it poisoned everything but it poisoned your family most of all.'

'But…if he said no to you marrying me and if you didn't need a marriage to seal the truce, then why let Thanasis and Lucie marry?'

'I didn't need the marriage but your family did. *You* did. I knew I couldn't press my wish to marry you without exposing our weekend together and causing you pain, but I couldn't walk away from the negotiating table without making sure you were protected. When my father refused to let Athena marry Thanasis, I nearly gave up, but I was able to turn him round to the idea of Lucie marrying him.' His laughter was a little less awful this time. 'I couldn't have predicted that encouraging their marriage would lead to such near-disastrous consequences for Tsaliki Shipping too, but it wasn't the business I was thinking of when I was so angry with your brother for confessing the truth to Lucie—it was you. It's always you. Everything I've done since that weekend has been for you.'

Turning his back to her, he poured himself another large drink. 'I prepared myself for the wedding. I knew I would have to avoid you. At that point I thought there was no future for me with you. You would never choose me over your family, I knew that, and I was trying to forget about you, but just hearing your voice…' His shoulders rose sharply. 'You called me a bastard. The first words I heard you say in three months was a rant to your brother about listening to *"that bastard Alexis".*'

He took another large drink then turned back to face her. 'And then you told me you were pregnant.' He shook his head and closed his eyes. 'I couldn't even process it. Not to start with. And your demand that I marry you? And you were so matter-of-fact and cold about it. The passionate, warm, affectionate woman who'd lodged herself in my heart had gone and you were treating me with the same contempt as your brother, and I was so angry with you for that. So fucking angry and wounded you would not believe. But you know what the worst thing is?'

She shook her head dumbly.

'When I demanded a real marriage, I was bluffing. I would have still married you if you'd refused it and given you the terms you wanted because there is nothing I wouldn't do for you. Even when I've been furious with you and hated you I would have still walked on broken glass for you.' The laughter that came from his throat this time was bitter and yet made her want to cover her ears and howl more than the awful nails-on-chalkboard laugh. 'I could walk on that broken glass and you'd still believe I was walking to someone else because you're too damned scared to trust me.'

She shook her head. 'I do trust you, Alexis, I do. You said that nothing happened with Angeliki and I believe that because you're not a liar.'

His voice hardened into granite. 'Your instinct is to distrust me. Your whole life has been spent hearing poison about my very name. You see what you want to see and believe what you want to believe. I know you have feelings for me. You're as jealous and selfish for me as I am for you but unlike you, my angel from Hades, I've not been running away from commitment,

I've been running to it but my running stops now because I no longer trust you. You clearly want out of this marriage…consider your wish granted.'

'What?'

'Don't look so shocked. This is what you want, and have I not made it clear enough that I would do anything you want? It just so happens that this is what I want too. When you told me you were mine, you didn't mean it.'

'I *did* mean it. When I married you I believed I was committing myself to you for life.'

'But you never really wanted it and you never believed I was doing the same.'

'Can you blame me? If you'd told me all this before then—'

'Then what?' he demanded roughly. 'Can you really put your hand on your heart and say you would have believed me?'

'We'll never know now because you never gave me a chance with the truth!'

'The truth about my love for you didn't need spelling out. It was there the whole time—you just refused to see it. You were never prepared to give the whole of yourself to me because of who I am, and you still won't. When you tell your parents about us, I don't want you making excuses for being with me and begging their forgiveness, I want you to stand proud beside me and tell them, *This is my husband, the father of my child, and I choose him of my own free will because I love him and nothing you can do or say will ever stop me lov-*

ing him. Can you do that, Lydia? Can you stand up to your family and be honest about your feelings for me?'

She shook her head in bewilderment. 'You know I can't do that. They would never forgive me.'

'And I know I will never forgive you if you don't. It seems I have my limits too. I don't want half-measures, Lydia, I want everything from you, your love, your faith and your trust, and I no longer trust I will have any of it, so I will settle for nothing because I never want to hate you.' The flicker of a smile played on his lips. 'As they say, it's the hope that kills you. Well, I'm out of hope. I will buy you a house like I originally suggested and put it in your name. Tell me what you want for maintenance and I will pay it. If you choose not to tell your family about our marriage then I will respect that but I will not—and let me be very clear about this—I will not be denied my role as our child's father. Once our child is born you will tell your parents that I am the father and I will be involved in his or her life and neither you nor your family, if they stand by you, will stop me.'

'I would *never* do that,' she said vehemently.

'Good. Then we won't have a problem.' He finished his drink, put the glass on the bar without looking at what he was doing, stretched his neck and strode to the door. 'I'm going out.'

'You're what? You're going out *now*?'

'I cannot be here when you leave so I'm going to check into a hotel with a fully stocked bar and get very, very drunk. I'll get my team onto finding a temporary place you can move into first thing in the morning, just until you find a home you're happy with.'

He really did want her gone, Lydia thought dimly, the coldness in her chest she'd barely felt until then spreading. None of this felt real, like she'd fallen into a waking dream.

He turned to face her with twisted lips. 'However, my advice to you is to return to your family. I would imagine that with the business saved they'll be in a frame of mind where they just might forgive you for sleeping with the enemy.' Now his whole face contorted. 'It's just a shame that you will never have the courage to fight to make them believe that I'm no enemy to them and that I have never been an enemy to you—but then, to have that courage you'd need to believe it yourself, and we both know you don't have any belief in me or courage in yourself.'

He closed the door softly behind him but the sound had the same impact on her as if he'd slammed it.

All the lights in the Antoniadis house were on, shadows flickering in the windows. The taxi driver one of the maids had called for Lydia drove past the dozens of cars parked outside and followed the driveway as far as it would go until he reached the small white cottage where the only illumination came from the outdoor sensor light.

Dressed in her usual slouchy top and jeans, the top button of which had refused to do up, she treaded heavily to her front door and let herself in. Once she'd paid the driver, who'd kindly brought her suitcases in, she gazed around at the walls that felt so much smaller than they had eight days ago.

Was that really all the time that had passed since she'd last been in her cottage? Only eight days? It didn't seem possible.

In her bedroom, she looked in the mirror and then, unable to bear the dullness in her eyes and the strange ashen colour of her skin, looked away, brushing her hair and tying it back without looking again at her reflection.

The noise coming from the main house filtered into the night air when she was halfway through a walk that felt twice as long as it ever had before, and suddenly it came to her that she was free. Free from Alexis. Free from a marriage she'd never wanted. Free from all those overwhelming emotions being with him made her feel: the jealousy, the possessive need, the tortured thoughts. Her family was saved and she was saved too. The plan she'd originally made to get through the pregnancy and then tell her family about her baby's father was viable again...

Her heart sank a little as she thought of the party she'd gatecrashed earlier. If they'd been seen arguing outside the house, then her brother would be bound to hear about it. What had *possessed* her to take such a risk?

She would cross that bridge when she came to it, she decided, and then smiled to know that within just two hours of her newfound freedom, she was feeling like her old self again. Alexis hadn't burrowed into her heart as deeply as she'd feared or as deeply as his arrogance had let him believe. Love? Oh, she'd come close to falling in love with him but she hadn't crossed the line from lust into love and now there was no danger that she ever would because she was free, and it felt fantastic, like the heaviest weight in the world had been lifted from her.

With a beaming smile on her face, she opened the kitchen door and stepped into the most raucous party she'd ever known her parents to throw. Fighting her way through the throng in search of them, a search that seemed to take for ever as all the partying guests knew her and enthusiastically embraced her, she thought every member of her family, her grandparents, aunts, uncles and cousins, and all her parents' friends and every senior employee of Antoniadis Shipping were crammed into the house celebrating the miracle.

'Baba!' She turned her head to find her mother elbowing her way to her from the dining room. 'You're back!' she cried, throwing her arms around her. After smothering Lydia's face with kisses she stepped back a little and cupped her daughter's cheeks. 'Let me look at you...*baba*, you look tired! Oh, this is such a lovely surprise—we weren't expecting you home until Sunday. Come on, let's find your father, and get you a drink and get some colour on those cheeks.'

Hands clasped together, Lydia let her mother drag her through the crowd to the kitchen where her father—she must have walked straight past him—was supervising one of the caterers in the making of a vat of punch by pouring liberal amounts of vodka into it.

'*Baba!*' he cried when he spotted them, and then Lydia was pulled into another tight embrace and her face smothered with a dozen more kisses. A glass of punch thrust into her hand, her parents raised their glasses and she followed suit, and when they both drank liberally, she kept her lips tight around the glass rim to stop any of the potent liquid seeping into her mouth. They were both too high on the euphoria of their business being saved to notice, too euphoric to notice too when Lydia discreetly switched her punch for an alcohol-free one.

'Is Thanasis not here?' she shouted over the noise.

'No, he's gone away with Lucie. They want some "time alone together".' Her mother rolled her eyes gleefully at this.

Lydia hardly dared to ask. 'Does this mean you are okay now about Thanasis loving her?'

Her mother threw an arm around Lydia's shoulder and kissed her temple. 'How could I not be? She has saved us and your brother loves her and she must love him too to have forgiven him for what he did to her.'

Hope opened its wings in her heart. 'Even though she's a Tsaliki?'

The glee on her mother's face deepened. 'But she isn't, is she? She was never properly one of those devil's spawns, and now she has turned her back on all of them to join the Antoniadis camp and hates them as much as we do, if not more!'

'If that doesn't call for another drink then I don't know what does!' her father interjected, his glee as evident as her mother's, and the wings of hope closed back up again.

Her fingers tightening around the glass, Lydia joined her parents in raising a toast to Antoniadis prosperity, and wondered why she'd even felt that hope. This was where she belonged. Here. With the people she loved and who loved her. Her family. She should be counting her blessings that Alexis had set her free. She *was* counting her blessings! Except...even in the haze of her euphoria, sickness roiled deep in her belly, and she didn't understand why she'd had to tighten her hold on the glass to stop herself from throwing the liquid in her mother's face or why she felt so strung out beneath her skin that there was every danger that one wrong word addressed to her would see her dissolve into a puddle of tears.

Alexis lay fully dressed on his hotel bed watching the early morning light filter through the curtains. Or trying to. The room was spinning. A whole bottle of the hotel's finest Scotch had finally kicked in.

Good. Let oblivion take him. Let him have this one night to wallow in misery and drink himself into a stupor. One more night of making terrible choices.

Lydia had gone. The message from his staff had come before he'd even settled into his hotel room. He'd laughed to read it. Of course she'd gone. The path of least resistance, that was Lydia's way. The only thing she'd ever fought for was their baby and he was the fool who'd let himself believe she would ever fight for him.

It had never been about him. If her family's business hadn't been so close to destruction he still wouldn't know she was expecting their child. She would have kept it a tightly wrapped secret because she was a coward. A coward who loved her family and was terrified of losing them.

She loved him too even if she couldn't—wouldn't—see it. But, as with the two fools who'd come before him, she didn't love him enough, and he was the arrogant fool to have let himself believe what she felt for him was different. If it was different then it wasn't a difference that was enough. Not for her.

He tried to drag air into lungs that no longer knew how to breathe for themselves. Better they end it now. He didn't want to hate her. Okay, he did want to hate her. He wanted to convince himself that his father had been right and that she was all the things he'd said the Antoniadises were the whole of his life. A scorpion.

He'd always known Lydia had a sting in her tail. She'd stung him the morning after their glorious passionate weekend together. He'd just never appreciated how deeply the sting would penetrate the second time it hit him, embedding so deep that he didn't know how to begin ridding himself of its pain. If half a bottle of brandy and a whole bottle of Scotch couldn't touch it then what hope was there for him?

Somehow, he needed to learn to navigate the rest of his life without her.

The darkness he craved was getting closer, his heavy eyes closing.

A solitary tear rolled down his cheek and then oblivion.

CHAPTER THIRTEEN

CLOUDS WERE GATHERING above Athens that early morning, the first break from the unremitting sunshine in over three months. Lydia took her seat amongst the extremely early-bird tourists and the first of the commuters and tried to shake the clouds gathering in the unremittingly sunny mood she'd determinedly retained for the past week.

The train set off. Moments later it stopped. Her heart clenched. A week ago, this was the stop she'd embarked at. It had taken her the full week to pluck up the courage to take it again and prove to herself that she really was over him; that there had never actually been anything to get over, that the madness of lust she'd found with Alexis was gone.

Don't think about him.

She'd been too busy to think about him other than in the abstract. Lydia had found a new energy. She'd thrown herself into her work, pitching for more contracts in a few days than she'd done in a year. No more picking and choosing the most exciting ones to catch her eye, now she was approaching her work like she always should have done, like a business and not like a hobby for a spoilt rich kid. If she'd approached it like this from the start then she would never have had to go crawling to Alexis when bankruptcy had loomed. She would already have been self-sufficient from her own endeavours.

Her parents had been too busy riding the wave of euphoria at the saving of the business to ask any questions about her time in London so she'd been spared from having to tell more lies. She never wanted to tell another lie. A few more days and she would tell them about the baby.

If anyone other than Helena realised she'd been the woman to leave the party with Alexis then they were being remarkably discreet. It looked like she'd got away with that moment of madness. She should be relieved but she was too numb to feel anything, and she still didn't know what she would say to her parents. Before, she'd planned to simply refuse to reveal the identity of the father until the baby was born and they'd fallen in love with their grandchild, yet whenever she tried to envisage the scene now, the sickness that had become a permanent part of her welled up and stopped her.

She couldn't leave it much longer. If they weren't so wrapped up in their euphoria they would notice her waistline had thickened. That morning, she'd caught sight of her naked figure and seen a small but detectable curve in her belly. Not quite a bump but definitely a precursor to one.

She'd come within a breath of calling Alexis to tell him.

There had been no contact between them. Not a call, not a message. Nothing. Radio silence.

She continued not thinking about him all the way to the Acropolis stop, all along her route on the Dionysiou Areopagitou walkway and past the church of St Demetrius, still not thinking about him when she disappeared through the trees onto the running route. The thickening clouds meant she didn't need to seek solace from the heat of the rising sun. But this was her route, the safe, comforting, familiar path she always took, and she pounded along it to the old quarry, still not thinking about him as she passed the crag and took the landscaped path to the top of the hill.

When she reached the marble Philopappos Monument, she took a long drink of her water and, before she could stop herself, she turned her gaze in the direction of the district where Alexis lived, easily seeking out his apartment block. She'd looked out at it from this very spot an average of five times a week since their weekend together. This was the first time she'd looked at it with dark clouds looming over it.

Was he there or had he already left for work?

Don't think about him.

Was he choosing which of his many, many, many snazzy suits to wear for the day?

Don't think about him.

Still unable to wrench her gaze from the direction of his apartment, she absently rubbed at her belly and the weird bubbling sensation that had just started in it...

Like flutters. Bubbling flutters...

Her eyes widened and she pressed harder. That was her baby. She could feel her baby. She could feel her baby!

Still pressing into her fluttering belly, she excitedly unzipped her side pocket and pulled out her phone. She needed to call Alexis. He needed to know this momentous milestone...

A fat raindrop fell on her nose. Another landed with a splat on her chin. In moments, the heavens opened with a load roar and seconds later Lydia was soaked to her skin, still holding her belly, water pouring off her phone.

Cursing, she wiped the phone on her soaked T-shirt and tried to unlock it but her fingers were too wet for her fingerprint to work and the deluge too heavy for facial recognition to work either. Excitement turned into panic. She couldn't remember the pin code she hadn't used since she'd first set the phone up. Hardly able to see at all through the waterfall of water, she tried every pin code she'd ever had, her need to speak to Alexis and share the news and hear his voice, right now, growing stronger with each failed attempt...

Her screen locked itself at the exact same moment the fluttering bubbles stopped.

'Please,' she sobbed to her baby, rubbing vigorously with one hand as she manically shook her phone in a futile attempt to bring it magically back to life. 'Please, do it again. Please. Please...'

Oh, God, she was crying, and no sooner had she realised her face wasn't just wet with the rain but with her tears, a keening wrench sliced through her chest, the greatest pain of her life ripping her heart in two and bringing her to her knees with a howl.

Call him? *Call* him?

Lydia didn't need to hear his voice. She needed *him*. Alexis.

She shouldn't be calling him to share the news. She should be there with him, living the experience with him, in his apartment, in the bedroom he'd turned into a beautiful sanctuary for her because he loved her. Alexis *loved* her. He loved her and she'd closed her eyes and ears to it.

She couldn't close her eyes and ears to it now. Each and every heavy raindrop fell on her like a mark of condemnation: condemning her for walking—running—away from him like a frightened child instead of fighting for them, and all because she couldn't handle what she felt for him and had never believed that she was enough for him; condemning her, too, for burying her head in the sand ever since, and all because the truth was too terrifying to contemplate, that to admit her real feelings for him meant admitting that she'd thrown away the best person in the whole wide world because she was a coward.

Another long, interminable day had bled into another long, interminable night, and now, with another long, interminable day to look forward to, Alexis stared out of his bedroom window at the torrent of rain lashing the streets. Finally, the weather matched his mood. Good. Why should he be the only one to suffer? The darkness of the rainclouds was nothing on the cloud that had lived in his heart since he'd returned to an apartment empty of Lydia.

She'd taken everything of hers. His cleaning crew worked such magic that not even a strand of her hair remained. The only item of hers he still possessed was the lipstick that had fallen in the back of his car that first night. He'd taken to carrying it around with him.

Time, they said, was a healer. *They* were liars. All time did was rip the gaping wound in his heart wider. He'd never imagined missing someone could be a physical pain.

How the hell was he supposed to move on when Lydia's ghost lived within the walls he slept in and in the very air he breathed? Somehow he had to find a way because this pain was beyond endurance.

The rain poured harder than ever but Lydia no longer cared. She lifted her face to it and accepted the drenching she deserved.

The safe, comforting, familiar path she'd taken on this run was the path she'd been taking all her life because she was too much of a coward to divert from it. Too much of a coward to forge a life, a real life, for herself. Too much of a coward to fight for the man she loved because she'd never had to fight for anything before, not even for herself. Yes, everything Alexis had said had been the truth, all except for one thing. She *did* believe in him. It was herself she'd never believed in. The great Alexis Tsaliki, a force of nature who burned brighter than the sun and who could have any woman he so desired, loved her. He wanted *her*. Just her. She was enough for him.

How could she have walked away after everything he'd done for her and everything he'd said? How could she have left him knowing that to leave him would be to destroy him? And destroy herself too.

She loved him.

The rain had stopped.

Lydia opened her eyes to the sun burning through the clouds. Its warmth bathed her skin.

She laughed and lifted her chin even higher. She loved Alexis. She loved him. She was his and he was hers, and she would do whatever it took, fight any fight needed, to make him understand and believe that she was his for ever.

Lydia let herself into her parents' house. Her running clothes were still damp from the rain but she didn't want to go back to her cottage and change, not until she'd done what needed to be done, now, before her father left for work.

They were both in the dining room finishing their breakfast, her father dressed in his suit, her mother still in her dressing gown.

'I need to talk to you,' she said without any preamble.

Her mother's lined face...the last year had seen those lines turn into grooves...furrowed. 'What's wrong, *baba*?'

'Before I tell you, I want you to know that I love you.'

'You're scaring me. Are you ill? Come and sit down. Petros, pour her a coffee.'

'No, no coffee for me, and I'm not ill, it's nothing like that, although I think you might prefer it if I was. I'm fourteen weeks pregnant with Alexis Tsaliki's child.'

Stunned silence.

Lydia opened her mouth and launched into the whole sorry story right up to the night she'd left Alexis, the only omissions the details no parent needed to hear about their child.

When she'd finished speaking, more stunned silence bounced loudly between the dining room walls.

After for ever seemed to pass, her mother rose unsteadily to her feet. 'Get out.'

Lydia closed her eyes, sucked in some air and ground her feet to the floor. Only when she was steady in mind and body did she open her eyes. 'I'm sorry. I know this is your worst nightmare come to life but Alexis isn't who you think he is—he isn't his father and he doesn't deserve to be blamed for his father's sins. If you want to thank anyone for saving the business, then it should be him. He's a wonderful man and he loves me and I love him, and he's going to be a wonderful father.'

'Get out and never come back.'

'I'll be out of the cottage by the end of the night.'

She'd reached the front door when a hand gripped her arm. 'He might not take you back,' her mother said with a viciousness that's sting was lessened by the tears in her eyes. 'And what will you be left with?'

Lydia smiled sadly. 'The knowledge that I fought

for him just as he's spent the last three months fighting for me.' And then she kissed her mother's cheek and walked out of the door.

Alexis approached the booth he'd slid into the first time he'd spoken to her.

Voices echoed.

'So, Lydia Antoniadis. Tell me why the youngest member of the family at war with my family is here alone in my hunting ground.'

'Catching my prey, of course.'

He could never have guessed in that moment how deeply and entirely she would catch him.

A hostess passed carrying a large bucket of chips. Just to see them and remember Lydia's love of them was another punch to his guts, and he made a sharp turn to the bar, unwilling to wait until he'd taken his seat at his personal booth.

He glanced at the tequila on the top shelf…

Only the good stuff.

'Get me a large Scotch,' he told the barman, and indicated for him to keep pouring until the liquid was a fraction from the rim. He drank half of it, looked at the remainder and then thought, to hell with it, and downed the rest before pushing the empty glass back to the barman and telling him to refill it. He hadn't touched a drop of alcohol since that first night he'd drunk himself into oblivion, though God knew he'd wanted to. It didn't numb the pain but, if he was lucky, it might numb his senses enough to get through a few hours of partying before he could make his excuses and leave, and return to a life now empty of all meaning.

Lydia climbed the wide, rounded stairs to the VIP section. The bouncer guarding the roped barrier checked her name off the list she'd maxed out her credit card to get on and let her through.

'Is Alexis Tsaliki here yet?' she asked with a brightness she had to dredge from the pit of her stomach to achieve. The Alexis she knew would never let a friend down—she doubted he had ever let anyone down in his life. He'd promised his friend he would host a party for him that night, and so he would be there to host it. Despite her knowing this, it still came as a relief when the bouncer nodded in answer.

This wasn't going to backfire, she told herself staunchly as she walked past the booth she'd hired all those months ago. Alexis *did* love her. If she had to have faith in only one thing then it would be that. The purest, most unconditional love in the world.

The dancefloor was packed and she had to elbow her way through it to reach the DJ.

Catching his attention, she rose onto her toes to tell him what she wanted.

He reared back and looked hard at her, as if satisfying himself that she hadn't just been released from an asylum, then turned his gaze to the direction of the most private of private booths before looking back at her.

She held the stare unwaveringly.

He inclined his head in dubious agreement.

She expelled a breath and smiled her thanks, then elbowed her way back through the dancefloor until she reached the exact same spot she'd danced at all those months ago and fixed her gaze at the club's most private of private booths, the one most hidden in the shadows, where a tall, well-built man with perfectly quiffed hair so dark it was almost black was holding court with his sycophants. Except, if it was a court he was holding, it was a court he didn't want to be at. His gaze was fixed in the distance. He didn't look bored. He looked vacant.

Her heart ballooned.

Why had he bothered to come? Alexis asked himself moodily. He should have stayed at home. The club's vibe was doing nothing for him, the incessant chatter and laughter of his friends and various hangers-on like sharp needles in his head. He couldn't even be bothered to drink himself into oblivion as he'd intended, his second full glass of Scotch mostly untouched.

He slumped back in the booth, lifted his face to the ceiling and closed his eyes.

'Anyway, Anastasia said...'

He tuned the voice out, would have inched away but was penned in. He didn't care what Anastasia had said. He didn't care about anything. Only Lydia. He should have been honest about his feelings from the start instead of expecting her to be a mind reader when he'd always known that she didn't believe him capable of being faithful and had known how much the thought of losing her family was hurting her. Where his feelings for Lydia were straightforward and uncomplicated, Lydia was not him, and he'd driven her away, punished her for not having the same faith in her feelings and in him as he had...

'I have a special request for Alexis Tsaliki.'

His eyes snapped open at the DJ's words echoing loudly through the speakers.

'Your wife asks that you join her on the dancefloor.'

A loud roaring noise filled his head, louder than the music, louder even than the sudden booming of his heart.

Hardly daring to believe what he'd just heard, Alexis slowly lowered his gaze.

A small curvy figure in a mid-thigh-length silver mini dress was standing directly in his line of sight on the dancefloor. Her blonde hair was loose around her shoulders, wisps of her fringe falling into her eyes.

Their stares locked.

Her chest and shoulders rose.

Slowly, she raised her arm and held her hand out to him.

Unable to tear his stare from her, not at all certain he wasn't dreaming this, barely aware that the people penning him into the booth had all fallen into stunned silence, Alexis rose to his feet and took the most direct route to the woman shining brighter than any strobe light by climbing over the table.

Lydia fought to keep her feet grounded, and keep her trembling hand held out to him.

Time slowed to a crawl.

There was not a flicker of emotion on his face and yet each slow step he took to her added to the emotions filling her so completely she could hardly breathe for them.

He stopped a foot away from her.

Her extended arm fell to her side.

The blue-grey eyes that had seduced her so completely from that first look bored into hers. The longing making her heart cry reflected back at her.

She took the final step to him.

With a tremulous smile, she palmed his cheek.

His lids closed in silent reverence before his stare locked back onto hers.

Bringing her face to his, she looked deep into his eyes. 'I have told my parents everything. They know I'm yours. Because I *am* yours. I'm yours, Alexis Tsaliki. Now and for ever.'

His jaw tightened. Long fingers caught the hand palming his cheeks. His breathing had become heavy.

She slipped her other hand around his neck and threaded her fingers through his hair. She could feel the tremors in his powerful body and dimly marvelled that this man, this titan of a man, loved her. Her.

'I love you,' she said, willing with every fibre of her being for him to feel her words and not just hear them. 'I love you, and there is nothing anyone can do or say that will ever stop me loving you, and there is nothing I wouldn't do for you. I would walk on broken glass for you, and I give my heart into your keeping of my own free will and I trust and have faith that you will keep it safe for ever because I am yours and you are mine and I can't go on without you.'

Alexis's fingers tightened around the dainty hand holding his cheek, his heart thumping so hard it threatened to burst through his ribs.

The hazel eyes gazing so intently into his filled with tears and then her voice broke. 'Please forgive me.'

Air expelled from his lungs in one long exhalation and for the first time in so, so long, Alexis found he could breathe. Bringing his mouth down to hers, he kissed her, closing his eyes and letting his senses fill with the softness of her lips and beauty of her scent.

'My angel,' he groaned before cupping her cheeks to stare into the eyes that were finally shining openly with love for him. 'You will never know how much I have longed to hear those words.'

Her arms slid around his neck, but the smile she gave still contained fear. 'Can you forgive me?'

With another groan, he brushed his lips to hers. 'There is nothing to forgive. You are my heart, Lydia, and I should have had more faith that you would feel the truth of it.' He rubbed his nose to hers. 'And more patience. My pride…my stupid pride pushed you away from me again. If you hadn't come to me tonight I would have come to you and got down on my hands and knees to beg you to come back to me. Forgive me?'

She sighed, and it was like she was expelling all the air from her own lungs in one long exhalation. 'There is nothing to forgive. Your impatience and pride are a part of you and you wouldn't be you without them.'

And then she smiled, and it was with such dreaminess that the last of his own fear turned to smoke and vanished. 'I love you.'

'And I love you.'

Her smile shone straight into his heart. 'Can we go home now?'

'As long as you're with me, I will go anywhere.'

Her lips fused to his in a kiss full of all the same passion and tenderness brimming in his heart. 'Then take me home and love me for ever.'

If the intercom hadn't been buzzing so incessantly, Alexis wouldn't have been woken from the best sleep of his entire life. Holding firmly to his wife, who was curled into him, he reached over to the bedside table and lifted the receiver. 'This had better be important.'

Once his butler had relayed the news, he muttered a curse and said, 'Let him in.'

Lydia lifted her head and sleepily asked, 'What's wrong?'

'Your brother's here.'

She blinked. 'What? Now?'

'Yes. He's refusing to leave until he speaks to me. You stay here. I'll—'

He never got to finish saying that he'd deal with Thanasis, for Lydia had shot off the bed as if she were turbo boosted, snatched her robe off the floor where she'd dropped it, and was shrugging her arms into as she stormed out of the bedroom.

Half laughing at this newly found terrier side to his

wife, Alexis pulled his discarded trousers on and followed her. He was halfway down the stairs when he saw her steaming over to her brother, who was standing by the apartment's main entrance.

'If you lay a hand on him then you and I are through,' she blazed, not letting him even open his mouth. 'So if that's what you've come here to do, then turn around and go. I love Alexis and he loves me. We come as a package now, so deal with it.'

Alexis stood behind her and wrapped his arms protectively around her waist while Thanasis folded his arms around his chest and arched an eyebrow. 'Have you finished?' her brother asked.

That nonplussed her. Folding her arms in turn, she nodded primly. 'Yes.'

'Good. Because I'm not here for a fight.' His eyes fixed on Alexis. 'My parents told me everything and while I will never forgive you for the way you treated Lucie, I love my sister and I want her to be happy.' His lip curled. 'Apparently she loves you and thinks you're going to be faithful to her, so if you can look me in the eye and promise that you *will* be true to her and that you'll always love her and take care of her then I will give you both my blessing.'

Alexis actually felt his wife go rigid in shock.

'Is this some kind of joke?' she asked.

Thanasis flashed a brief smile at her. 'No joke. I have no wish to lose you over this bastard and I'd very much like to be a part of my niece or nephew's life, and I know our parents want the same too.' His smile dropped. 'They love you. Just give them time. It won't be long, I promise.' His gaze fell back on Alexis. 'Well?'

'I love her,' Alexis told him, not wavering. 'And I meant every word of the vows I made before God.'

For the longest time, Lydia held her breath as she watched her brother eyeball her husband. Whatever he saw in Alexis's stare must have convinced him of the truth for the hardness in his eyes softened a touch and he extended a hand to him. 'Welcome to the family.'

Hardly able to believe her eyes, Lydia watched her husband and brother shake hands, and then a moment later she was being pulled into her brother's embrace. 'Be happy,' he whispered fiercely.

'I am.' And knowing she had her brother's blessing and that her parents still loved her completed it for her.

He kissed the top of her head and then turned to leave. 'I'll be in touch.'

'Thanasis,' Alexis called as he was closing the door.

Her brother looked back.

'Tell Lucie I'm sorry.'

The ghost of a smile played on Thanasis's lips. 'You can tell her yourself at our wedding.'

With the door closed, Lydia looked at Alexis. He met her stare and cupped her cheeks, disbelief apparent on his handsome face. 'Did that just happen?'

She couldn't hold back the beam a moment longer and then, just when she thought her happiness couldn't be more complete, fluttering bubbles thickened in her belly…

'Our baby!' Tugging Alexis's hand down to her abdomen, she pressed it tight to the place where the flutters were happening. 'Can you feel it?'

His gorgeous eyes lit up with wonder. 'That's our baby?'

'It is!'

He shook his head in awe. 'God, I love you.' And then he kissed her and carried her up to their bedroom to show her exactly how much he loved her.

EPILOGUE

LYDIA SPIED ON her father, making sure he didn't put the whole bottle of vodka into the vat of punch. Noticing her, he winked, tipped a little more in and then screwed the lid back on. Standing behind him, egging him on, was her father-in-law.

Grinning, she weaved her way through all the guests into the huge kitchen, where her mother was supervising the caterers unloading all the party food. The plentiful surfaces were practically groaning under the weight of it all.

'Come on,' she said, sliding her arm into her mother's elbow. 'This is a party. You're supposed to be enjoying yourself, not working.'

'But I don't want you having to do anything, *baba*—it's your celebration.'

'That's why we have the caterers here, and, as Alexis owns the company, they're going to do an extra specially good job for us, so please, let them get on with it and come and enjoy yourself.'

'It really is a beautiful house,' her mother said as they wandered through to the main reception room.

'You're just saying that because we're only two minutes away from you now,' Lydia laughed. When she'd been in hospital giving birth to their second son, their oldest son, Matthaios, had stayed with her parents. When they'd collected him the next morning and found him playing football with his grandfather and uncle in the sprawling garden, they'd both known the time had come for them to buy a family home with a garden for their children to play in. Six months later, they were finally settled in and throwing their housewarming party for it, both families coming together in another celebration.

It had been amazing how magically babies worked at dissolving family feuds, and while Lydia's mother would never make a friend of any Tsaliki apart from her son-in-law, she politely tolerated the others and pretended not to notice the rekindling of her husband's friendship with Georgios. Lucie, too, who had more reason than anyone to hate her stepfamily, had found motherhood softening her attitude to them and had recently rekindled her relationship with her own mother.

This all made Lydia very happy. Family was everything to her and as far as she was concerned, the more in it, the merrier.

Once all her guests were settled in and enjoying themselves freely, she went back into the kitchen and helped herself to an enormous plate of chips, then sneaked out through the back door into the garden and into the balmy summer air. There, she followed the path to the tree to the left of the swimming pool. Waiting for her beneath it was the person who made her the happiest of everyone.

Alexis saw her and grinned, and raised the bottle of tequila he'd sneaked out and the two shot glasses.

Let their guests entertain themselves. They were going to have their favourite kind of party—a private party for two.

* * * * *

Did His Pregnant Enemy Bride
*sweep you off your feet?
Then don't miss the first instalment in the
Greek Rivals duet*
Forgotten Greek Proposal

*And why not explore these other stories
by Michelle Smart?*

Cinderella's One-Night Baby
The Forbidden Greek
Heir Ultimatum
Resisting the Bossy Billionaire
Spaniard's Shock Heirs

Available now!

HARLEQUIN
Reader Service

Enjoyed your book?

Try the perfect subscription for Romance readers and get more great books like this delivered right to your door.

See why over 10+ million readers have tried Harlequin Reader Service.

Start with a Free Welcome Collection with free books and a gift—valued over $20.

Choose any series in print or ebook.
See website for details and order today:

TryReaderService.com/subscriptions

RSBPA24R